# Secret Baby Daddy

An Enemies to Lovers Second Chance Romance

Josie Hart

Copyright © 2024 by Josie Hart.

All rights reserved.

This is a work of fiction. All of the characters, organization and events portrayed in this story are either products of the author's imagination or are used fictitiously.

No part of this book may be reproduced in any form or by any electronic or mechanical means, including information storage and retrieval systems, without written permission from the author, except for the use of brief quotations in a book review.

# Contents

1. Layla — 1
2. Luke — 9
3. Layla — 16
4. Luke — 23
5. Layla — 31
6. Luke — 37
7. Layla — 44
8. Luke — 51
9. Layla — 58
10. Luke — 65
11. Layla — 74
12. Luke — 79
13. Layla — 87
14. Luke — 94

| | | |
|---|---|---|
| 15. | Layla | 101 |
| 16. | Luke | 108 |
| 17. | Layla | 115 |
| 18. | Luke | 122 |
| 19. | Layla | 129 |
| 20. | Luke | 136 |
| 21. | Layla | 143 |
| 22. | Luke | 150 |
| 23. | Layla | 157 |
| 24. | Luke | 164 |
| 25. | Layla | 171 |
| 26. | Luke | 178 |
| 27. | Layla | 186 |
| 28. | Luke | 195 |
| 29. | Layla | 202 |
| 30. | Luke | 209 |
| 31. | Layla | 216 |
| Epilogue - Luke | | 222 |
| About the Author | | 229 |

# 1

## Layla

"Is that...is that Luke Whiss?" My champagne glass fell from my lips as I took in my old flame's caramel hair and chiseled physique. His skin was tan and face freshly shaven, showing off his square jaw and perfectly positioned dimples in each cheek as he laughed.

*Jeez, he only gets hotter with age.*

"Who?" Xavier, my new acquaintance, whipped his head around to stare at the man stealing all of the oxygen from the room.

"You know him," I snapped, squeezing past him and Delilah.

"Where are you going?" My best friend grabbed my arm. "I know you said you had a history with him, but I didn't think—"

"I just don't want him to see me," I said quickly, wriggling from her grip. There weren't many places I could run, considering we were out on a yacht, miles from shore.

"Did you not see his name on the guest list?" Delilah called after me. "I emailed it to you."

Shaking my head, I continued across the deck, unable to rip my eyes from Luke. It was as if he felt me staring, because he turned his head in my direction...

And *oof*. Our gazes locked and my stomach swirled with apprehension.

He turned on his heel, heading right in my direction, but I backpedaled, running right into the railing. It hit just below my butt, and I felt myself flipping backward...

*Oh shit, I'm going over. I might die.*

I shut my eyes as people around the yacht gasped; however, the splash into the water below never came. I felt a firm grip on my wrist, and when my eyes fluttered open...

There he was.

"Well, that would've been a spill for the books," Luke chuckled, pulling me forward. My sandals slipped on the wet deck and I fell in the opposite direction, landing on his chest.

*Ugh.*

That old familiar scent of sandalwood hit my nostrils like a burst of happy gas, dulling all my common sense. It was as if time froze in that moment...

And I was suddenly dragged back to ten years ago, when Luke had called everything off.

*Fuck.*

I pushed the heartache away and pushed myself off his chest. "Sorry about that."

"Shouldn't you be thanking me?" He raised an eyebrow at me, his eyes twinkling under the sun as an amused smirk crossed his face. "You could say that I just saved your life. It's a long drop from up here."

I cleared my throat, hardly able to meet his eyes. "I would've been just fine, thanks. I've fallen further," I lied. The closest I had come to going that far was when I was once drunk enough to jump off a small cliff into a lake.

He burst into laughter that my mind took as mockery. "You have *not* fallen further, Layla. You're terrified of heights. I highly doubt you picked up cliff diving in the last...what? Five or six years?"

I glared up at him. "A lot can change in *six* years."

*Like having a daughter.*

Something flashed in his eyes, his smirk fading. "I'm sure it can." His tone was flat as he let out a sharp breath. "Didn't expect to see you at this vacay thing."

"So you didn't know that your best friend's wife is *my* best friend?"

He looked surprised by the statement. "No, I have to say that's news to me. Since when are you Delilah's best friend?"

"Since we met a year ago," I answered him, gaining some confidence. After all, the last time he and I had been together, *I* was the one who left. I folded my arms across my chest, trying to appear indifferent as my insides grew stormy.

"Wow, I can't believe Jett didn't tell me..." His voice trailed off as he glanced back at his high school best friend, now gulping down a beer. "Actually, I *can* believe that he wouldn't have told me. If I had known you were here..."

"You wouldn't have come," I finished with a scoff. "You don't have to pretend to be cordial with me, Luke. We all know you hate my guts. Might as well have let me fall off the stupid boat."

He laughed. "Right, and why would you even come to that conclusion? You're the one who blocked me on literally *every* fucking social media site known to man."

"I prefer to keep my exes where they belong," I snapped. "In the past."

"*Ooh,* what a burn." He snickered. "What are we? Back in middle school?"

*Ugh.*

I rolled my eyes, feeling more childish than even middle school. My eyes drifted back to Xavier, who was watching me with a curiosity that was almost embarrassing.

"You know you really should stay away from him," Luke said in a low voice. "There's a reason we didn't hang out with him in high school."

"Yeah, because he was two years younger than us, and our class was massive." I eyed Luke regardless, seeing his upper lip twitch slightly.

"He's nothing but trouble."

"Yeah, and you're not?" I retorted, handing him my now-empty champagne glass. "See ya around, Luke."

"You know you will. This is an all-inclusive trip for the next three weeks."

"Yeah, yeah." I waved him off as I walked away, letting my face fall as I left him standing there. I knew that my ass looked phenomenal in my black cover-up for my bikini.

*Let him stare.*

I had worked hard on my physique after having my daughter, putting in countless hours at the gym and watching everything that went into my mouth for a solid year afterward. Granted, I had relaxed in the last year and a half, but I still stayed in good shape...

And I hoped that Luke noticed.

"Well, that could've been really bad," Delilah said carefully, eyeing me. "And I saw things were tense..."

"Everything is tense with a guy like Luke Whiss." I blew it off, hoping that Delilah wouldn't ask any more questions. She knew that there was a past between Luke and me—and that it wasn't good—but

Jett hadn't filled in the details like I thought he might, and there was no way I was going to offer it up.

"I wouldn't know," Xavier spoke up. "I was never cool enough to hang with you guys back in high school. Funny how you can be rich enough to attend a fucking high-priced boarding school, but still not fit in."

"Well," I sighed, "I wasn't rich, and I didn't fit in great either. I only got in because my mom was a teacher and I was *gifted*."

"And now we're talking about high school like it wasn't ten years ago." Delilah giggled. "Shall we discuss who was the prom queen that year as well? Because while you lovely lucky people were kicking it at some high-society high school, I was attending a public school in the middle of nowhere." Delilah brushed her dark hair out of her face. "I had to marry up into this world."

"And I had to work my ass off to get here," I added, giving her a smile. "This is why we're best friends."

"True, very true."

"I like a hardworking woman." Xavier offered me a second glass of champagne as the tray came by.

"Thanks," I muttered, taking the glass from him. I didn't want to admit it to him, but it was the biggest turnoff *ever* when a guy only saw me for the dollar signs around me. It was like PTSD.

I never liked my worth to be wrapped up in money.

But that was the world we lived in, and I hated it. If it weren't for my best friend being a part of the high-society crowd, I would *never* be caught dead in a place like this.

All thanks to Luke Whiss.

*Ugh. Asshole.*

My eyes drifted across the deck to where he was standing, chatting it up with two women I didn't know. But I *did* know they were models, clients of the talent agency that Jett owned. That was how he'd met Delilah—but unlike Luke, Jett didn't judge her for her lack of societal standing.

Luke's eyes looked past one of the women, locking with mine. Heat flooded my cheeks as I quickly diverted my gaze. He was like a car wreck—a very hot one—that I couldn't look away from.

"Is Autumn staying with your sister?" Delilah's voice brought me back to the conversation.

"Uh, yeah, she is." I felt my chest tighten at the mention of my daughter. "This will be the longest I've been away from her since she was born."

"How old is she?" Xavier asked, seemingly unbothered by my single mom status.

"She's five," I said carefully, taking a deep breath. "Well, five and a half, really. She starts kindergarten this next fall."

"Aw, I love kids." Xavier beamed. "Do you have any pictures? I bet she's a cute kid if she takes after you at all."

I chewed the inside of my cheek as I dug my phone out of my cross-body purse. I didn't want to even make a remark to Xavier on that topic—because Autumn looked like her *father*. "Here." I clicked the lock screen, my daughter's face filling the background.

"Man, definitely a cute kid," he said, leaning toward me to get a better look. "She's got your eyes."

"Yeah, she does," I said, letting out a breath. She might have my green eyes, but Autumn had her father's caramel-colored hair, olive skin tone, and dimples—and yet even being the spitting image of her father, *no one* had ever put two and two together.

Not even Delilah and Jett.

Well, actually, there was a part of me that thought Jett might be suspicious, considering he'd asked me once who her father was—and my answer had been shaky at best. Ever since then, he hadn't asked, but I caught him staring at her any time I took her to their house. Honestly, I was playing a *dangerous* game, but somehow I'd told myself it was okay, because Luke lived in NYC and never came around Jett's place anymore.

"So, are you staying in one of the suites at the resort?" Xavier asked me, a flirty smile on his lips.

*Keep dreaming, buddy.*

"Everyone is," Delilah chimed in, answering for me. "I got an adjoining suite with Layla though."

I nearly choked on my champagne as I held back my laughter at the look on Xavier's face.

"You two really are something," he grunted, shaking his head. "But for the record, I wasn't trying to invite myself over or something."

"*Right*," Delilah giggled. "I know what kind of guy you are—always jumping from woman to woman. Layla might not know your reputation, but I do."

He shrugged, unbothered. "It's not like the ladies turn me down. I'm a high-caliber man."

"Uh-huh, I bet you are," I teased, loosening up a little as I poked his shoulder. I could suddenly feel Luke's gaze boring into the side of my head, and I had no problem working this scene in my favor—even if Xavier was getting nowhere.

"See, she's not *that* against me." He wiggled his brows. "Though, I have to admit you're not really my type. I'm more into the blonde, Cameron Diaz type."

"That's a very specific type," I laughed, downing the rest of my champagne.

"Everyone's got one," he leveled with me. "But I do occasionally make exceptions for the hot underdog kind of brunettes that nearly fall off of yachts."

Okay, that one got me.

Delilah and I both burst into laughter, and while I let myself get lost in the casual flirty giggles, I glanced over at Luke...

He was *seething,* his lips in a flat line and jaw clenched so tight it was visible from across the deck of the yacht. I smiled slyly at him, tipping my empty glass in his direction.

*There's the jealous alpha I've always known.*
*Let the torture begin.*

# 2

## Luke

"She's already fucking with my head," I growled to Jett, having dragged him inside to the main cabin of the boat. "Why the hell did you not tell me she was coming?"

Jett let out a heavy sigh. "Because if I told you, you wouldn't have come, and I haven't seen you in like, eight months. It's nice to get to see you in person for once. I get tired of the shitty late-night phone calls."

"Yeah, well, I have to work," I snapped. "And I still might've come if I'd known she was going to be here—I just would've been better prepared for my head to be fucking *shattered* at the sight of her."

And *fuck,* was my head frazzled. She was hotter than ever, her long, tan legs poking out of a sheer black cover-up. Her dark hair, creamy skin, and bright green eyes were still just as captivating as ever. I'd nearly gotten an erection just *seeing* her.

"Look, the last time you saw her was what…six years ago, right? I mean, I get that you two were together all through high school—but it's been *ten years* since you were a couple. I'm not an idiot, and I know you both took it hard..." His voice trailed off for a moment as he glanced out the window to the rolling waves. "But we're adults now. She's my wife's best friend. Delilah wouldn't have even wanted to do this if Layla wasn't here."

"Yeah, well..." I couldn't even argue with that point. I *should* be over Layla. I'd honestly thought I was—not that I had been with anyone since that night in the city six years ago.

And shit, that was embarrassing to think about.

"I know it's a shell shock to the system, seeing your ex, but we've all got exes. It's just a little nostalgic when you see them. A lot changes in ten years." Jett ran his fingers through his blond hair, and I could tell by his tone that he was desperate to smooth this whole thing out. He was a mediator—and a people pleaser. He just wanted everyone happy...

And no drama.

"You know, it's that night six years ago that makes it sting so much, seeing her." I hated making the admission, but it was the truth, and Jett was my best friend...

He needed to understand why I would be taking off when we landed back at the marina.

"Yeah, I know that night was rough on you."

"She left before the sun even came up." I replayed the morning in my head, waking up to find Layla gone. I had thought it was the beginning of a second-chance romance for us, but instead it was just the beginning of a second tumultuous heartbreak.

"You really need to let that go," Jett grunted, unenthused. "You're the one who broke her heart first, and exes fuck up and sleep together after it's over all the time. I couldn't let go of my ex until I met Delilah.

She changed it all for me. You just need to find your Delilah—then Layla will just be a woman of the past."

"Right." I didn't feel like arguing that Layla was *way* more to me than Brittany had ever been to Jett, but whatever. "But anyway, I was just letting you know that I'm gonna probably head back to the city when we get back in."

His jaw dropped. "Are you fucking serious? All because *Layla* is here? Luke, there are nearly forty people here for this—and plenty of eligible singles. Don't leave, man. I've been looking forward to spending time with you for months."

"Yeah, and I can't have a good time if she's here. I can already tell she's going to play games with me." My chest burned with frustration as I said the words. "That's what she did to me in NYC, and she was purposefully flirting with *Xavier* earlier to make me jealous. It's just fucking stupid."

Jett's annoyed expression was a slap in the face. "There's no way in hell that Layla is trying to play games with you. That's *you* doing that to yourself, reading into shit that's not there. It's been years, and I highly doubt she's out to mess with your head. You *always* do this when it comes to her. You create all these narratives that turn her into the villain, and all it does is drive you crazy."

My jaw tensed at his words. It wasn't the first time he'd said something along those lines. "I just don't want to be miserable the entire time. She'll just fuck with my head, and then I'll be in a horrible mood the whole time."

"Well, first of all," Jett chuckled, "you're *always* in a bad mood. And secondly, *if* she's playing games with you—and I *really* don't think she is—you going back home is just letting her win. You have to show her that you're unbothered by her being here. That's the best revenge you can give, right? Being indifferent and living your best life?"

"So you're a life coach now?" I shot back at him, wincing at the glare he gave me.

"No, but I don't want my best fucking friend bailing just because his ex from *years* ago is here. If I had known it was going to be *this* big of a deal, then I would've just figured something else out. I didn't tell you because I thought it wouldn't matter. You haven't mentioned her in a really long time. I thought you were over her."

*Yeah, because then I might come across as pathetic.*

"It'll be fine," I muttered, feeling like an idiot for being so bothered. "I think it's just a reminder of how burned I was."

"I get that." Jett held up his hands. "But again, it was years ago. Layla's really made some big changes in her life. She's got a kick-ass cosmetics company that's brought her a ton of success. She's made her own way in the world without the help of anyone."

The thought intrigued me, not having known about any of her life in the last six years. After the night in NYC, she really had blocked me on every platform imaginable, and no one was willing to fill me in on how she was doing.

Which is why I apparently had *no* idea she was best friends with Delilah.

But then again, Jett had only met Delilah a couple of years prior, and their relationship had moved faster than the speed of light, leading to them eloping in Hawaii without anyone knowing. I guess that was true love or whatever.

"Luke?" Jett waved his hand in front of my face. "You okay? If you really wanna go, I'm not going to make you stay here. I just don't think you should take off so quick. At least give it a few days, then if it's still too much, leave."

I let out a sigh, straightening the white Columbia fishing shirt I had on. I wasn't much of a beachgoer, so I'd done the best I could with what I already had. Of course, now that Layla was here, I was wishing I would've done a little better.

"I'll stay for now," I muttered, not remotely comforted by the relief filling Jett's face. "But I'm *not* having anything to do with Layla."

"Okay, well, she'll keep my wife busy, and you and I can just focus on catching up. I'll introduce you to the others who came." Jett waved me back toward the staircase that led to the main deck.

"Yeah, speaking of people you invited, why the hell is Xavier here? I get that he owns a string of VIP nightclubs, but I never knew you were friends with him." There wasn't necessarily anything wrong with the guy, though I had heard he could be shady in his dealings...

And for that reason, he'd better stay the fuck away from Layla.

"We use one of his clubs as basically a studio for the models. It works out really well, and Delilah finds the guy intriguing—not in a romantic way, of course."

"Right, well, I'm sure he's got plenty of women at his fingertips."

Jett chuckled, pushing the door open for me. "You give him way too much credit, man."

Just before I stepped out of the interior cabin stairwell, Jett and I both froze, hearing the sound of a sputtering engine.

"Uh...you got a motor problem?"

"*Fuck*," Jett mumbled. "I swear the engine in this thing is trash. I've paid more on mechanics than I paid for the entire boat. If Delilah didn't love this thing so much, I wouldn't even own it anymore."

"So we're gonna be stranded out here?"

"Nah, I'll get it running. You can go ahead and head out. I'll get this." He shooed me out. "Just don't let Delilah know that I'm fighting this dumb thing. She doesn't want to get rid of the boat, but she's also terrified of being stranded out here."

"Complicated," I said under my breath as I stepped out into the setting sun. I took in the sight of the endless water on the horizon. It was a nice evening off the coast of Miami, and don't get me wrong, I could appreciate the scenery.

It would just be a lot better if I didn't have Layla fucking with my head.

My eyes scanned the crowd, but she was nowhere to be found, thankfully. I wandered to the railing, leaning against it as I peered down. It *would've* been a long way to fall had she really gone overboard.

*I would've jumped in after her.*

"Fuck me," I chided myself, rubbing my jaw. No matter how much I disliked the woman, I knew I wouldn't hesitate to be there if she needed me...

"So, the billionaire recluse actually showed up, huh?" Xavier's hand landed on my shoulder. "I had forgotten what you looked like after all these years. You don't look much like your brothers or father."

"Yeah, I guess that's how I fly under the radar so well," I answered him through gritted teeth. "It's not really my thing to be in the public eye, anyway. Eli does that well enough."

"Mmm, yes." Xavier sipped his drink, squeezing my shoulder before dropping his hand to the rail. "I saw his wedding in People Magazine. Beautiful, cinematic event. It was very fitting for the owner of a media production company."

"That was his wife's doing, but yeah," I chuckled, pushing away the tinge of jealousy that came with the thought of my older brother's wedding. He and his wife seemed to have it all made, like they were just some meant-to-be fucking love story, complete with a baby now.

"You sound a little bitter." Xavier gave me an amused look. "Your old flame got you feeling that way?"

*Fuck, I could push this guy overboard right now.*

"All good," I said, finding comfort in the thought of his cocky smirk hitting the waters below.

"She's single, you know." There was something in his tone that ground every single fucking nerve in my body. The thought of his hands on her curves...

"You probably shouldn't try anything on this trip." It came out as more of a warning than I had intended, but Xavier only laughed.

"Ah, yes, the overprotective ex. What a story, yeah? I've dealt with them before and..." He paused, leaning in toward me. "I can deal with it again. It just makes the chase a little more exciting."

I stood up straight, bumping my chest right into him. "Oh, I bet it'll be real fuckin' exciting." My Boston accent dropped, and Xavier stepped back.

"Guess we'll see." He shot me a wink before heading back to the crowd.

Now I definitely couldn't go anywhere. I needed to be here to keep that creep away from Layla.

*Mission accepted.*

# 3

# Layla

"Thank god," I groaned as I shut the door to my suite behind me. Being out on the yacht had been fun, but after the whole incident with Luke, I was over it. I'd spent the rest of the time hiding out in one of the rooms with Delilah, creeping on Luke's social media. I hadn't looked through his profiles in *years*, vowing to myself that I would never go there again…

But yet, there I was.

He didn't really post much—if anything at all. He wasn't like the rest of his brothers, enjoying every ounce of the spotlight given to them along with their fortune. His brother Eli was the *biggest* playboy. Well, until he settled down. But even now, he and his wife were in the limelight. And Jackson? He was a *rock star*. So naturally, it just made sense for him to be plastered everywhere. However, I couldn't say much about him…

I did own all his albums.

I plopped down on the bed, my head hitting the soft bedding behind me. I had considered leaving, just cutting my losses and heading home. But then, that would let Luke win.

And I was not about to let him win again.

Taking a long breath, I glanced at my smartwatch. I only had a couple hours until the evening party that apparently *everyone* was going to. Delilah had made it out to be a social hour, full of dancing and all that jazz. It sounded like a bad idea, and I wasn't exactly the biggest partier, considering I spent most of my free time with my five-year-old daughter. Parties these days required princess dresses and tea, not martinis and dirty dancing.

*But maybe I should let loose.*

If there was one thing I knew about Luke, it was that he was a *jealous* guy. He always had been—starting fights with any man who stared at me a little too long. A shiver of excitement rolled through my body at the thought, moisture pooling between my legs.

*Ugh. Stop it.*

I pushed myself up into a sitting position and decided I would just bide my time with getting ready and looking as hot as possible. I wanted to show Luke that I wasn't the same poor, nerdy girl he'd dated in high school. I was *rich* and I was *sexy*.

At least, that was what I told myself in the mirror every morning.

Laughing to myself like a psycho at my own joke, I headed to the bathroom. I stripped out of my cover-up and bathing suit, pausing to check myself out in the mirror. I'd had a boob job after Autumn was born, and it was a good thing…

Because now was the time to put them to good use.

I spent the next hour getting ready, carefully doing my makeup in nightlife style. I focused on a good smoky eye but natural airbrushing. I'd never worn makeup in high school because it had caused me to break out horribly—which is actually why I'd developed my own products after college. I'd just had no idea they would take off the way they did.

Slipping into a tight, black bodycon dress with a steep v in the front exposing a plethora of side boob, I headed back to the bathroom to finish my hair. I left it down in loose beach waves, my dark locks falling past my shoulders. I had gotten a spray tan before coming to the vacation, but it didn't amount to much, my skin only a little *less* white.

That being said, I still looked *hot*.

And that was exactly what I was going for.

I still had a good thirty minutes before the party started. I considered banging on the door to the adjoining room and bothering the shit out of Delilah and Jett, but based on the faint noises coming from the other side...

It was probably best that I not.

Instead, I grabbed my phone, scrolling to my sister's name. I hit the call button, hoping to catch Autumn before she went to bed for the evening.

"Hey!" Lily, my older sister, greeted me as the screen filled with her face. "I was wondering when we were going to hear from you. You've only been gone like a day, and Autumn is already asking when you'll be back."

"Aw, no." I frowned, my heart squeezing. "Is she already in bed? I know it's almost seven-thirty, but I figured she'd be staying up late at your house."

"She's still awake, but right now she's watching a movie with Kody," she referenced her own six-year-old daughter. "I don't want to disturb them while they're actually being quiet for once. You look *hot*. What's the plan for this evening?"

"Um, they're having some kind of party at the nightclub here in the resort. I'd much rather be there watching a movie though."

"Oh stop." She waved me off, laughing. "You need to get out and have a little fun. It's been years since you've gone on vacation without Autumn. Moms deserve to let loose, you know."

"Yeah…" My voice trailed off.

"What is it?" Lily asked me, tilting her head. Her bright green eyes reflected mine, but she had dyed her hair blonde—and it had been that way for years.

"You'll never believe who's here…" I couldn't even meet her eyes on the screen.

"Um…" She paused, appearing to be in deep thought before her mouth dropped open. "No…"

"Yeah…I thought Jett didn't really talk to him anymore, since they've been living here in Miami, and Luke's in NYC, but nope. I almost fell off the boat when I saw him…*literally*."

"Oh my god," she gasped, shaking her head. "What if he finds out about Autumn?"

*She must've missed the part about me actually nearly dying today.*

"I don't know how he would. No one knows who the father is except for you, Mom, and me."

"You don't think Jett can see the resemblance?" I could hear the concern in Lily's voice, and it made me feel more anxious than I wanted to admit.

"I don't know if he can, but he hasn't said anything to Luke as of yet, so I don't know why he would now."

"Ugh… You know, maybe you should've just told him all those years ago. It's like a ticking time bomb since you're so close to Delilah. All it takes is for Luke to see a picture of Autumn—and I think he'll know."

"I don't know…"

"You know how much she resembles Luke, Layla. The math is pretty obvious, too."

"It was just one night," I argued. "He couldn't even remember the exact amount of years it had been when I talked to him today."

"Mmm." Lily gave me a face. "He's such a jerk."

I held back the automatic urge to defend him—even though I had no reason to. "He can be. I just know that I'm going to be staying far, *far* away from him on this trip."

"Well, good luck, because you look *fire* tonight, and you're gonna turn all the heads in the room with that ensemble." She laughed, and I was relieved to see her relax. "I can't believe you're still single, really. You know Nate would be more than happy to set you up with one of his friends when you get back—and before you tell me no, I really think you should consider dating."

"I know, I know," I grumbled. "I just don't like trying to mix dating with parenting. It's so hard. Plus, guys are assholes."

"So be a lesbian."

"I don't think it works like that," I giggled. "Otherwise, I would've changed years ago."

"Right, well, I hope you have a *great* night, and flirt with all the hotties there. Maybe snag an exotic guy for the night—but wrap it this time, yeah?"

"Shut up!" I burst into laughter, shaking my head at her. Over my laughter, I heard a familiar sweet voice in the background.

"Is that my mom?" Autumn asked from a distance. "I wanna talk to her!"

A huge grin spread across my face as I saw my messy-headed daughter appear on the screen. She had a smile on her face as she took the phone from my sister.

"Hey, honey, are you having fun with Kody?"

"Yeah! Are you having fun?" she asked, tipping the phone back so I could only see the top of her head. I laughed at her face being so close to the screen.

"I'm having fun, but I already miss you." My heart thudded in my chest as I thought about what Luke was missing out on...and anytime I let myself think about it, the guilt came moments later.

*But it's for the best. He wouldn't want to have a kid with someone like me.*

I wasn't ever good enough for him, and having a kid wouldn't change that. There was a chance his big fancy family might try to take custody away from me or something...after all, he had kept everything about our relationship a secret for that very reason.

"I love your hair, Mommy. You look like a princess," Autumn said into the phone. "Do you think you could do my hair like that when you get home? Kody doesn't like to play tea party like you do. I want to go to a ball like a real princess too."

I laughed. "Well, I bet Aunt Lily would do your hair like this if you ask her to."

"I would!" Lily called from the background. "I can do *great* princess hair."

"Ooh..." Autumn giggled. "I want my hair done like Ariel. Can it be red too? I *love* red hair."

"That's a tough order, but maybe you can figure something out tomorrow. You probably need to go to bed soon."

"Aunt Lily said that we can stay up late tonight and finish the movie."

"Oh, well, I guess if Aunt Lily says so—"

"Oh! I need to go eat my popcorn!" Autumn cut me off. "I love you, Mommy. Have fun at your tea party."

"Thanks, honey," I laughed as the phone dropped to the ground, leaving me staring at the ceiling of my sister's house. A few moments later, Lily appeared, picking it up off the floor.

"Sorry, I swear kids just throw these damn things around like it's nothing. I'm seriously surprised my phone isn't broken yet. Kody chucks it across the room when she's done watching Blippi. You'd think she was preparing for softball or something."

"Well, you did play in high school."

"I was terrible at it," she shot back, giving me a look. "But seriously, have fun tonight, and try not to worry about Luke. He's just one asshole in a world full of many. It's not worth the heartache to let yourself go there—also, you probably shouldn't sleep with him."

"What?! Why would I do that?" I nearly choked on air. "I have *no* interest in going there again." *Even if my body still thinks I do.*

"I don't know...I feel like he's always had a hold over you, no offense. I just don't want to see you getting your heart broken again. He's nothing but bad news."

"I know, I know," I reassured her. "You don't have anything to worry about. I have no interest in going backward."

"That brings me very little relief," she said, laughing half-heartedly. "But yeah, have a nice time tonight."

"Thanks, maybe make sure Autumn is in bed before nine?"

"No promises. We're living our best life over here, watching The Little Mermaid for the third time today."

"Oof, jealous. Talk soon." I hung up the phone, dropping it onto the bed beside me. My eyes drifted toward the door, my heart racing at the thought of seeing Luke tonight...

*Just keep your head on straight, Layla. You can do this.*

# 4

## Luke

*Will she even show up tonight?*

I leaned against the bar, my eyes focused on the doorway. I wasn't sure why it mattered if Layla showed up to the late-night party or not, but it was all I could fucking think about. It was a nice club, but it was overdone, looking like a tiki bar mixed with a rave—an impossible conversation that left my head pounding.

"*Bro*, why are you just standing there like a dud?" Jett clapped his hand on my shoulder. "You look like either you're about to fall asleep or you're just really unhappy to be here."

*Is there an option for both?*

Honestly, I was exhausted. My bedtime rolled around at like nine-thirty. I wasn't the kind who to be out late-night partying anymore. I had a set routine that I lived by: work, gym, dinner, read, bed. And I did everything in my power not to deviate from my schedule. I preferred to live my life that way.

"Luke!" Jett snapped his fingers in my face. "Are you seriously going to ignore me? Are you still pissed that Layla's here?"

I whipped my head in his direction. "Nah, I'm not mad at you. I'm just tired."

"Ah, yeah, I forgot that you're literally an eighty-year-old man in the body of a twenty-eight-year-old." Jett chuckled to himself, downing the rest of his drink. "You really should let loose while you're here. You'll miss out on a lot of fun going to bed at nine-thirty."

"No one said I was going to bed then," I retorted, rolling my eyes. "We used to go out all the time."

"Yeah, and you were a party pooper back then too. I can't even think of a time when *you* were the life of the party."

"I don't want to be the life of the party." I reached for my drink, my eyes scanning the room for any sign of Layla. I'd been watching Xavier closely, and while he made himself out to be interested in Layla, he was caught up with a couple of models...

And I hoped he stayed that way.

Layla was too good for him—even if she was...whatever she was.

"You need to drink about five more of those, and maybe you'll actually smile." Jett chuckled to himself before drifting off into the crowd. I stayed where I was, having no interest in socializing. I knew I was no fun at this kind of shit. The only time I'd ever let myself get lost in a party was back when I was with Layla...

And that night in New York City six years ago.

I tried to put it out of my mind, to push the humiliation and heartache away. Layla would always be the one woman who just...*fucked me up*. And her timing was perfect—in walked the siren herself.

And *fuck*, I was hard in an instant—and *pissed*.

Her breasts were nearly *falling* out of her dress, leaving little to the imagination as she stepped into the club. The red strappy high heels accentuated her taut calves and the dress only came to her upper thighs...

*Easy access.*

Was she trying to get to me? I knew I shouldn't give myself that kind of credit in her life...since she was apparently doing much better without me. Still, I couldn't help but rake my eyes over her figure, picturing her bent over, my cock *deep* inside of her...

*Stop, Luke. She's not worth the fucking pain.*

But I couldn't get my brain in working order as those potent eyes locked with mine. She acted like she was heading right for me...

And then she tapped Xavier on the shoulder.

*What the fuck?*

I growled as he turned, his eyes making the same pass that mine just had, his entire expression full of nothing but pure lust. He left the models, grabbing Layla's hand and pulling her out onto the dance floor.

*Why is she letting him dance with her?*

My chest was boiling with an anger that I hadn't experienced in *years*. I understood that Layla was a single woman, free to do whatever the hell she wanted...but Xavier? Nah, that wasn't going to happen.

"I need two more of these." I motioned to my drink as the bartender gave me a funny look. I downed it—and the next two, giving myself all the liquid courage necessary to do what needed to be done.

And then I stalked right out onto the floor where Xavier was moving in rhythm with Layla. His hands weren't on her yet, but I knew the game—and I knew that they would be before the first fucking song was over.

"Luke!" Jett called, but I ignored him, lightly tapping Xavier on the shoulder.

"I'm gonna cut in here," I said, keeping my tone flat.

"Uh, you might want to make sure that's what the lady wants?" Xavier shot back, giving me an annoyed look.

"Just thought we could catch up," I said to Layla, giving her a warning look that I *knew* she recognized.

She let out a sigh. "Yeah, that's fine. We can *catch up*."

"You don't have to do whatever he wants," Xavier said to her in a soft, sweet tone that would make someone think I was a controlling prick of an ex-boyfriend.

And well...maybe I was.

"It's fine, really," Layla muttered, stalking off the dance floor and heading to the bar.

I followed her, my third drink in my hand. "Where are you going?" I demanded.

She made it to the bar and spun around to face me. "Well, if I'm going to have to deal with *this*"—she motioned to me—"all night, then I need a hell of a lot more to drink."

"Wow, so I'm really that bad, huh? You really wanna spend the night with that asshole?" I didn't hide my irritation, taking a step closer to her. "He's a womanizing, conniving, shady—"

"No," she cut me off. "You're just saying that because you don't want to see me with anyone else."

"And why would that even fucking matter? I don't give a shit who you fuck, Layla," I seethed, leaning in closer to her. "I was just trying to look out for you."

"Oh, well, *thanks*." She rolled her eyes. "You were *so* sweet to go interfering with my night before it even got started. Just *amazing*."

"You know, you should be more appreciative."

She burst into laughter. "Appreciative of what? My jealous ex-boyfriend ruining my vacation before it can even start? How *selfish* of me."

I gritted my teeth. "I was *trying* to keep you from making a mistake."

"I think I've made plenty of those," she said, her voice nonchalant, which only made me even *more* angry as I knew *exactly* what she was talking about. Before I could say anything else, she pushed herself off the bar, shaking her head. "You know what, Luke? This isn't even worth it. You don't want to catch up, you just want to lord over me, like always."

My mouth dropped open as she headed toward the club exit, her ass making a fucking scene with the way it swung on her way out. I stalked after her, chasing her out the door and back into the resort.

"Where the hell are you going?"

"To my room," she shot back, punching the elevator button. Layla flipped her dark hair over her shoulder, showing me a glimpse of her prominent collarbones.

*Fuck, fuck, fuck.*

My dick was hard again as the elevator doors opened. She stepped inside, her eyes meeting mine in a way that set the world on fire around us. *This* is what we always did—we fought like hell and then we fucked even harder.

"Go back to the club," she said in a low, sultry voice, hitting the door close button.

My arm caught the door, and I stepped inside. "I'll make sure you get back to your room then."

Her lips parted as the door closed, and suddenly...we were alone. Layla's chest rose sharply, and my eyes drifted down the steep neckline to her perky breasts.

"Never seen you in something like this..."

Layla's tongue ran along her bottom lip, her eyes stuck on mine like she was in a trance. "I...I thought I would let loose tonight."

"Hmm..." I took a step toward her, realizing that the elevator hadn't moved. As I leaned in, my nose inches from hers, my cock throbbed and her breath hitched. "What floor is your room on?"

"Fourth floor," she panted, and I already knew that regardless of how much she hated me, I *still* got under her skin.

And that was the biggest fucking turn-on.

I ran my fingers along her jaw, my heart rate picking up speed as I made it to the tiny dimple in her chin. I leaned in a little further, noticing the flush in her cheeks...

And then I punched the fourth-floor button.

The sound of her disappointed sigh was enough to tell me everything I needed to know. Spinning back around, my hand threaded through her hair and I pinned her against the wall with the force of my body.

And then she kissed me.

Her kiss was hot and fucking desperate as she ground her hips into my erection, letting out a cute little whimper as she did. Nipping at my bottom lip once, she then sucked my tongue into her mouth, forcing me into every inch of her mouth. I let out a groan, my free hand running down her side to the hem of her dress.

I *needed* to know how wet she was for me.

"*Ooh.*" She let out a moan as my lips left hers and quickly moved to her neck, my fingers trailing up her thigh, feeling the lace of her underwear.

"So fucking accessible," I groaned as soon as I brushed her wet center. "You were just asking for trouble in this dress."

"Was I?" she teased, meeting my eye in a playful way.

I growled in response, pushing her underwear to the side and sliding my fingers between her wet folds. "You're so wet for me, Layla." I rubbed her clitoris, loving the way she clenched her body around my touch. It might have been years since I'd fucked her, but I still knew her body like the back of my hand—and I knew what she liked.

"*Ugh, Luke...*" She tipped her head back against the wall as I slid a finger inside of her, going for the same spot I always did.

And then I dropped to my knees.

Using my free hand, I pushed her dress up around her waist, revealing a black lacy thong and creamy skin. I didn't want to think of the men who had been here after me, fucking the pussy that was first *mine*.

I was gonna make her forget them all.

*Payback.*

Holding her underwear away, I spread her legs further, not even bothering to kiss my way to her clit. I just fucking buried my head between her legs, my tongue replacing my thumb, allowing me more freedom to finger-fuck her.

"*Oh. My. God.*" Her hips rocked against my face as I gyrated my tongue against her. I knew how to make this woman cum. *I* was the one who had first brought her this ecstasy.

Layla kept rocking, her fingernails buried in my scalp as I brought her closer and closer to the edge. I lapped up every fucking ounce of moisture she gave me, alternating between circling her clit and stroking the space between her pussy lips. Her legs trembled as she let out a moan, filling the elevator with the sound of pure pleasure.

"Oh *fuck*!" she cried out, before pushing me away. I stood to my feet, my cock throbbing to take her. Suddenly reality came rushing back when I glanced at the elevator door, standing wide open. We had arrived at the fourth floor...and I had *no* idea how long we had been putting on a show for whoever might've walked by.

I turned back to see Layla tugging her dress down, shaking her head. She glared up at me before storming past me and into the hallway.

"I can find my own room, thanks," she snapped.

"You're seriously just going to walk away after that?" I asked, exasperated, following her down the hallway.

She stopped in her tracks, spinning to look at me. "We *both* know that shouldn't have happened—and it *won't* happen again."

I raised my brow at her, letting her go. Moments later I heard a door slam, and I knew she had made it to her room. I ran my fingers over my face, the taste of her still lingering in my mouth...

*Why the fuck can't I stay away from her?*

# 5

## *Layla*

"Why am I so stupid?" I asked myself in the mirror as I wiped the makeup from my face. I had made myself up for a solid night out, and instead I'd spent freaking fifteen minutes in the club...

And the rest being devoured in the elevator by my savage ex-boyfriend and secret baby daddy.

*Fuck me.*

I had gotten so caught up in the moment, lost in the way Luke made me feel. As much as I wanted to tell myself I hated him, he knew how to make feel sexier than anyone else ever had.

*Because he was the first.*

"*Ugh.*" I tossed the makeup wipe in the trash and peeled my dress off my body. My pussy was still throbbing, still coming down from the high he had given me. It had been almost *six* years since I had cum because of anyone other than myself—and Luke had brought me to ecstasy in a matter of minutes.

It made my stomach sick to think about our history and all of the heartbreak that had gone with it. I tossed my underwear into a pile with the dress and headed to my room. I dug out an oversized black tee and a fresh pair of underwear, then fell onto the bed. I wasn't one to stay up late, so it was actually a relief to be in bed at a decent time.

I closed my eyes, Luke's face instantly filling my vision. A groan escaped my lips at the thought, wondering had we been somewhere else—somewhere other than an elevator—if I would've let him put his cock in me...

*No. I stopped it because it's a bad idea. I know better.*

But my own thoughts weren't very convincing as I lay there in bed, trying to think myself to sleep. My mind just wouldn't shut off, the past hammering me with all the regret and heartache.

The sound of a knock on the door caused my eyes to flutter open, and I sat up, halfway wondering if Luke had come back to explain what the fuck that had been about in the elevator. He had started the moment—even if I had been the one who kissed him first. My bare feet padded across the bamboo floors of the suite, and I leaned forward, peering through the peephole.

*Delilah.*

She stood just on the other side, her hand on her hips, clad in a red clubbing dress. I already had a good idea as to why she was here. I unhooked the chain and swung the door open.

"What the hell are you doing already going to bed?" she demanded, storming past me into the room. "I didn't even see you tonight—and then Jett mentioned you leaving with Luke? But I saw Luke literally ten minutes ago, chatting it up with the bartender."

*Of course he fucking was.*

Jealousy threatened to overshadow the wall I had built, but I brushed it away, forcing a smile. "I was there this evening, but I got a headache and decided to come back to my room."

She narrowed her eyes at me, folding her arms across her chest. "So, I would totally buy that, except that Xavier said you ran out of there, clearly in a fight with Luke. Jett said the two of you didn't end great, but I didn't realize just how fucking *savage* your relationship was."

"It's not *savage*," I corrected her, though honestly I wasn't sure. Maybe we *were* a little over-the-top—but there was just *so* much hurt beneath the surface...

At least for me anyway.

He had dropped me like I meant fucking nothing, and I was able to move past that as long as I wasn't face-to-face with him...

Or as long as his face wasn't buried in my pussy.

"Look, we're best friends, but what the hell happened with him? Jett wouldn't tell me anything, saying that it was none of his business and that he didn't want to get involved with any of the drama."

"I won't let there be any more drama," I promised her. "I'm so sorry. I just haven't seen him since...well...it's a long story."

"Okay, well, *please* enlighten me as to the last time you saw each other—and why it feels like there's a war in the making on a friendly vacation. This is supposed to be fun for all of us."

I plopped down on the edge of the bed, letting out a heavy sigh. "He broke up with me the day before he left for college after our senior year of high school. I kind of knew it was coming, but I guess it didn't keep me from hurting. He hid our entire relationship from his family. I was devastated—and he never answered my phone calls."

"Brutal... How long did you date?"

"Um...we started dating the week I turned sixteen, so like two and a half years." I hated recalling those years of my life. He had literally consumed every thought back in those days, so when I thought of high school, I only thought of him.

"Okay, so then you quit talking? I thought you mentioned seeing him like six years ago or something?"

"Well, I took a trip back to NYC to visit some of my old friends. I thought he had moved—he always said he wanted to live in LA, and his last social media post had shown him in Maui with some of his friends..." My voice trailed off as I thought about venturing back into the city where my heart was broken.

"But he was back in the city."

"Yeah, he was there with his brother Eli at the same bar that I was at. He saw me and approached me like nothing had ever happened between us." I paused, recalling the way it had felt to see him for the first time in so long. "It was almost like coming home? I don't know. I mean, I *was* home, but I fell right back in love with him. We spent the entire night together, laughing and catching up. He made it seem like there was a chance for a future or something."

Delilah's gaze turned sympathetic. "Oh my god, I'm so sorry, Layla. I had no idea he broke your heart like that. I would've put up a fight and told Jett not to invite him. I mean, Jett was honestly surprised he even showed up."

"It's fine. I left him that night, anyway. I crept out of his flat just before daylight. I took a cab straight to the airport and flew back to Miami. I knew he was going to break my heart again. I was stupid for letting him in, so I blocked him right out of my life. It might've been cruel, but I had to do it..."

*Because I was pregnant.*

"Did he ever try to call you?" Delilah asked, tilting her head. "Or did he just let you go like nothing happened? Because you know, you might've left, but he *could've* made the chase."

"Nah, he didn't. I think it made him really angry." I laughed, though it wasn't because I thought it was funny at all. "That's what Luke does. He just gets mad and bitter. He never actually admits to feeling anything. Not anymore."

"Yeah, Jett says he's the epitome of Mr. Scrooge. I didn't know what he meant until I met him when we took a trip to New York. Like, holy shit, he was literally the worst host. I don't know how someone as bright and sweet as you could put up with that level of grump."

I shrugged, fighting back the emotions threatening to creep in again. "I don't know. I guess he wasn't always like that. He was a big dreamer back in high school, and he made me all these promises—promises that he didn't keep," I added, shaking my head in disgust.

"All because...what? You weren't rich? I think that's what you told me."

"Yeah, he comes from a family of billionaires and socialites, and I come from a family of middle-class workers. I think his family wants him to be with someone of some sort of social standing—or something."

"Okay, but isn't his brother just married to a writer?"

"Yeah, some super successful one. I don't know. I have no idea. Maybe that's just what Luke wants."

"Well, he obviously hasn't found it—and Jett said that you've been all he's focused on since he saw you on the yacht. He might be a jerk, but he's definitely zeroed in on you."

"Obviously not if he's chatting it up with a bartender."

"Nah, men are dumb. They do shit like that to play it off like they don't care. One time Jett went and flirted hard-core with a photographer while he was trying to get my attention. It was super pathetic, and I think he creeped her out on accident, but you know, he tried."

"Yeah, he's not smooth at all." I laughed, feeling a little lighter at the subject change.

"He's an idiot is what he is. Sometimes I have no idea how he's come so far with this whole talent agency thing. He's the most unorganized guy ever, and he's so kind that he hates turning anyone away—even if they have no talent."

"Maybe he just sees the diamond in the rough," I suggested, glancing over to my phone. I tapped the screen to see what time it was—and if there were any notifications. For some reason, I thought there might be something from Luke...

*Like he has my number.*

*And I didn't just leave him in the hallway.*

"Don't worry about Luke," Delilah said softly, patting my forearm. "You're gorgeous, and *so* successful. You've come a long way since he last saw you, and I know we've only been friends for like a year...but I know you deserve better than some guy who leaves you high and dry—or makes you feel anything less than fucking perfect. You need to find your Jett."

I nodded, swallowing the lump growing in my throat. For the longest time, even after Luke had left, I had continued to think he was the one—that someday he would come back and apologize for leaving me the way he did...

But he didn't.

And then when we'd met up again, he'd acted like it had never even happened. It was like I was just supposed to ignore the fact that I wasn't good enough for him back then.

"We're having breakfast downstairs in the morning," Delilah said to my silence. "Why don't you join us? Xavier will be there. I mean, he's literally the *worst* choice, but you know, you can always just use him as a distraction. He won't even mind."

I laughed, ignoring the familiar pang of heartache forming in my chest. "I've never been much of a flirt."

"Well..." She gave me a sultry look, wiggling her eyebrows. "Maybe it's time for Miss Layla Miller to step up her game."

# 6

# Luke

"This is fucking incredible," Xavier groaned as he shoved a bite of his breakfast into his mouth. I didn't even know what it was, really, but it appeared to be a parfait of sorts. Either way, he was being dramatic over some yogurt...

And his presence was just annoying.

"Where is Layla?" Jett asked from beside me, his eyes zoning in on his wife. "You said she was going to be joining us this morning."

"She is..." Her voice didn't sound confident. "I bet she's just running late." However, the way she stole a glance at me told me everything I needed to know.

*Layla confided in Delilah about what happened.*

It triggered irritation, but at the same time...if it kept Xavier from coming on to her, then all the better. I was well aware that I was a jealous prick—I always had been. I didn't like what was mine to even be *looked* at by someone else...

*But Layla isn't mine.*

I cleared my throat, downing water and pushing away the thought that reminded me of just how hollow my chest was these days. I had to remind myself that Xavier just wasn't a good guy...

And I was just looking out for Layla.

"Ah, there she is!" Delilah beamed, her whole demeanor shifting as she looked past me.

I wanted to turn in my chair and lay eyes on who I *knew* was walking up behind me, but I forced my eyes toward my plate of fruit and pancakes. My stomach knotted up as Layla pulled out a chair adjacent to me, putting Jett right in between us...and as soon as I stole a glance, taking in her ample breasts spilling out of the top of a halter-top sundress, I knew I wasn't going to be eating any more of my breakfast.

"How'd you sleep?" Xavier asked Layla, his dark eyes lighting up at the sight of her.

I kind of wanted to rip those eyes right out of his head.

"I slept really well—like a baby." Layla smiled this sickeningly sweet smile in his direction, her white, perfect teeth sparkling. "How'd you sleep?"

"Same, pretty much. Well, I would've slept a little better had our night not been interrupted." Xavier threw a glance in my direction.

*I could take this asshole.*

Instead, I only grunted, forking around some of the strawberries on my plate.

I heard Layla take a sip of her coffee; the rest of the table had gone quiet. "Maybe we could make up for it today?"

I dropped my fork, and it clattered obnoxiously on the plate.

"That would be nice, yeah." Xavier got a wicked smile on his face, and I clenched my jaw, feeling Jett's eyes boring into my skull.

"I have a mechanic coming to look at the yacht today. I guess maybe we just don't take it out enough or something. Either way, hopefully we can get it fixed. The whole point of this vacation was to use the shit out of it."

"I'm sure Ronny will fix it," Delilah said in a soft tone to her husband. "He's the best of the best when it comes to boats."

"Yeah, and that's what you said the last time, and here we are again," Jett grumbled back to her.

As much as I hated seeing Jett upset about the yacht, I was also relieved that the conversation at the table had shifted—for now, anyway.

"I mean, we can always hang out on the beach," Layla offered up, her voice causing me to look up from my plate for longer than a split second. She met my gaze with confidence, and I hated to admit it but...

Damn, she was knocking me down a few pegs.

"I like that idea," Delilah chimed in. "We can have a solid game of beach volleyball or something. Not to mention, I have a few books I'd like to read too."

"I could stand to splash around in the water," Xavier added. "And I'm sure everyone else will be more than happy to join us."

"*Mostly* everyone." Layla let out a chuckle, shooting me a smirk.

"Oh, I'd *love* to join," I shot back, giving her the fakest fucking smile I had.

"I bet," Layla scoffed, rolling her eyes at me.

I couldn't take it anymore. "Take any long elevator rides this morning, Layla?"

"Do *not*," Layla growled, looking like she might jump across the table at me. "The only long elevator ride you'll be taking is the one to your *funeral*."

"That makes no sense." I busted up laughing.

"Literally, *none* of this makes sense," Jett said, his tone flat. "Who the hell wants to take a long elevator ride, anyway? Those things freak me the fuck out on a good day. I was once on my way to a meeting when mine got stuck for nearly seven hours. It wasn't even the claustrophobia that got me—it was just the heat. The AC went out in it."

I blinked a few times at my best friend, his awkward reply leaving everyone at the table staring at him.

"What?" He shrugged. "I'm sure plenty of people don't like elevators."

*I happen not to mind them when great pussy is involved.*

"Yeah, I don't really like them," Xavier added in a cool voice. "But if Layla likes to ride elevators, I guess I would be willing to hop on."

*The fuck you would.*

"Nah." Layla shook her head. "Luke was just referring to the fact that my elevator was a little slow last night—when I left because of a headache."

Delilah gave her a weird look, but then quickly replaced it with a smile. "Oh yeah, I reported that to the front desk this morning for you. They need to know before it gets worse—and then someone actually might get stuck."

"You didn't—"

I saw the nudge under the table, Delilah clearly pegging Jett with a solid bump to the calf. Did they think they were being discreet? And why even be discreet? People get drunk and shit happens. Everyone knew Layla and I had a history, right? Who gave a shit if it caught up to us a little last night?

*Oh, wait...is this about Xavier?*

I glanced over to the guy, eating his parfait in the most oblivious manner. There was no way Layla could seriously be interested in this dopehead...

"Yeah, so the mechanic is supposed to be here this morning around ten-thirty. I'll have to go out and get everything ready for him. Do you wanna join me, Luke?" Jett gave me that *you better fucking say yes* look, but I shook my head.

"Nah, I think a game of beach volleyball sounds better."

Layla nearly choked on her coffee, and I had to bite back my laughter. This was going to be a fucking phenomenal day. I could already tell.

"Well, if that's the case..." She dabbed at her mouth with a napkin. "I better go change into something a little more appropriate for beach volleyball." She shoved herself back from the table, giving me the worst glare ever.

And it was such a fucking turn-on.

Oh, and it was annoying. But yeah.

"See you out there, Layla," Xavier called after her.

"Yeah, see ya, *Layla*," I echoed him, chuckling.

Delilah shot me daggers as Xavier picked up his empty breakfast container and headed toward a trash can. "Can you seriously not just be nice?"

"What?" I raised my eyebrows like I was actually surprised.

"Don't badger him," Jett grunted. "It's fucking awkward enough as it is. I should've known better than to put the two of them in the same state."

Delilah shook her head as Xavier came back, taking his seat and looking around at all three of us.

"Did I miss something?"

"Not at all," I said in an overly sweet tone. "I'll see ya on the beach."

With that, I pushed my chair back, and the timing was perfect as my phone started to ring in my shirt pocket. I pulled it out, not surprised to see my brother's name on the screen.

"Hey, what's up?" I answered, heading toward the door of the restaurant and slipping out into the resort lobby.

"How's your vacay going?" Jackson asked me, letting out a chuckle. "Seems fuckin' crazy to say that to you, you know. Out of the entire family, you never take them."

"Uh...it's going." My eyes darted around, looking for Layla—not that she'd be here. She was apparently getting ready for beach volleyball.

Whatever that entailed.

"Yeah, okay. Well, that makes it sound like you're having a *great* time. Anyway, I wouldn't have called and bothered you, but I was hoping to talk to you about something."

"If it's about me making your New York show, I already told you that Eli and I will be there."

"It's not about that at all, bro. I know you'll be at the show. I already sent you your VIP shit." He chuckled, though it sounded like it was more from annoyance than anything else.

"Okay, so what is it you wanna talk about?"

"Let me get Eli in on this," Jackson said, and I heard the other line ringing. It wasn't close to Dad's birthday, so I was at a loss as to why I was suddenly in on an impromptu family conference call.

"What's up, bruh?" Eli answered in a stupid Cali-surfer voice on the other end of the phone. I swore ever since he got married to a dork, he was slowly becoming one himself.

"Hey," I grunted. "Looks like Jackson has something to talk to us about."

"Oh shit." Eli's voice suddenly went flat. "I already told him we'd be at his show."

"I *know* that!" Jackson let out a groan. "This is something totally different."

"It's not Dad's birthday for another few months," Eli pointed out the same thing I had been thinking. "There's no need for us to be planning anything right now."

"I don't know why you two always think you have me figured out. I'm clearly unpredictable as fuck."

"No, you're still the same old little brother you always have been," Eli chuckled. "But okay, tell us what's on your mind."

"Okay, so you know the record label, Y2K?"

"Uh...isn't that *your* record label?" I furrowed my brow, taking a seat in one of the empty chairs in the lobby. My gaze drifted out to the blue waters, and as much as I was dreading the beach volleyball thing, it *was* a pretty view.

"Well, it's the label that I'm signed to. It's not actually *mine*."

"We know that," Eli quipped. "We're not stupid."

"Never said you were—though sometimes I wonder," Jackson shot back, but then laughed. "Anyway, the owner is wanting to put it up for sale..."

"No, I'm not buying a record label," I instantly replied. "That just sounds like a whole lot of drama. I know how you *creative* people are."

"I'm listening," Eli said, causing me to roll my eyes.

"I think all three of us should go in together to buy it," Jackson said with a sigh. "And I know that you don't want drama, but you wouldn't have to have any, Luke. You could just be a silent partner if that's what you wanted."

"It could grow Whiss Productions." Eli was starting to sound more positive than I expected. "Let me think about it. Send over the information and I'll take a look."

"You want me to send it to you too, Luke?" Jackson asked.

I was hesitant, but as the middle child, I did *not* like being left out. "All right. Yeah. Send it over. I'll at least look it over."

"Cool! This is gonna be rad. Nothing like having a bro-owned business."

*Cringey as fuck.*

I shook my head. Maybe at least this would give me a distraction from Layla.

# 7

# *Layla*

"All right, I need the truth." Delilah let out a sigh as she plopped down into a beach chair. The two of us had made it oceanside faster than the rest of the group.

And now, I wasn't sure that was a good thing.

"What do you mean?" I played dumb, sitting down in the lounger beside her, a book in hand. "You know—"

"No," she cut me off, holding up a manicured finger. "It was made clearer than ever at breakfast this morning that you and Luke still have something going on."

"What do you mean?" I shot back, narrowing my eyes at her. "We were a long-term relationship that he hid from his parents—"

"What happened on the elevator, Layla?" she cut me off again. Delilah *always* saw through bullshit, and I should've known this would be no different.

"Ugh..." I ran my fingers through my loose dark hair, thankful for the umbrella shading the two of us. "Okay, so he *might* have gone down on me in the elevator—but I just lost my head for a second—that's all it was." Admitting it out loud made it sound even worse than it did in my head.

"*Girl*! No wonder he was so fucking brutal at breakfast!"

"Yeah, and I kind of just left him cold and went to my room," I added, cringing. "But in my defense, all he's ever done is break my heart, Del. I have to...protect myself." It sounded so pathetic, but it was the truth...which is why I had kept Autumn from him.

"Ouch..." Her face contorted. "That makes so much sense though. Maybe you should lighten up on things with Xavier. I was all for the game, but..."

I shook my head. "He fucking *destroyed* me, and he acted like it was *nothing* to him. It was just *poof*! Suddenly we couldn't be together, and we weren't worth telling his parents about."

She nodded, giving me a sympathetic smile. "Yeah, I get that...but also, I think there's something more on his end. What kind of guy gets *that* grumpy over someone he doesn't care about? Men are dumb, yeah, but he's being over-the-top."

"But that's just how Luke is," I groaned, leaning against the back of the chair. "He gets all possessive, but he never actually *wants* me."

"This is complicated." She breathed out a heavy breath, pushing her sunglasses up on top of her head and looking me dead in the eye. "Is there *anything* else I should know about the two of you—because if I'm going to be here for you, I need to know it all."

I bit my lip, wondering *just* how good of a best friend Delilah would be if she knew my biggest secret. "I...okay." I sighed. "I do have *one* more thing."

*Might as well get it out.*

"But you can*not* freak out—and you have to promise that it'll stay between us. Like, you can't even tell your husband."

"Oh my god," she groaned. "What did you do, Layla? I mean, of course I promise not to tell and all that—but I can't promise I won't freak out. That's just not fair."

"Okay, okay." My heart picked up its pace in my chest. I hadn't told *anyone* other than my parents and sister about Autumn—and I hoped more than ever that I would be able to keep this from backfiring.

"You have to tell me." Delilah leaned toward me, squeezing my forearm. "I promise I can handle it. If you knew the secrets of my family, you'd have no doubt about that."

"Your fam is crazy," I laughed, finding a little comfort. Her dad was rumored to be associated with an underground drug ring, so honestly, I bet she *did* have some dark secrets. She might not be high society like her husband—but there was still *something* going on under the surface of her past.

"Okay, so what is it? I'm ready." She shrugged her shoulders and pursed her lips, eyeing me with anticipation.

"Autumn is Luke's daughter." I spit the words out before I could change my mind, and *fuck,* did it come out sounding as terrible as I felt about it.

She nodded, silent for a few moments. "And he doesn't know."

I gave her a sheepish look. "Yeah...it's bad, I know."

Her head tilted back and forth as she chewed her lip. "Uh...I mean, there's worse things out there, I guess. Plenty of men probably have kids they don't know about. The difference is that you're face-to-face with him right now."

"Yeah, but I haven't been until now."

"But he's my husband's *best friend.*"

"I know, and I *think* Jett might already have his suspicions about it."

"My husband is literally a genius, but I can guarantee he is absolutely oblivious to shit like that."

"Well, I guess that makes me feel better," I said, though I wasn't sure it did. I wasn't sure that Delilah knowing made it any better either. However, she was taking it *way* better than I expected.

"So have you considered telling him?" she asked, glancing around us like he might just show up out of nowhere. "Because he does have a lot of money, and Autumn would get a huge chunk of that being his kid."

"Maybe, except she's also half me, and he might not want anything to do with her at all. I don't even know if Luke is a kid person. He might cut her out of his life, and that would be so painful for her."

"This is true, but what are you going to do when she's old enough to ask those super hard questions? She might take off looking for him when she turns eighteen. I had a friend in high school who did that. She didn't have a billionaire for a dad…but yeah, it was still a big deal to her."

I nodded, swallowing the lump in my throat. "I've thought a lot about that kind of thing, and I know eventually I'll have to tell her…I just don't want her heart to be broken like mine."

The sympathy on Delilah's face made me feel like a pity case. "Oh Layla, I'm so sorry. Your secret is safe with me, and I'm so sorry we're on this vacation. If I had known about all this, I would've begged Jett not to invite Luke—or we could've done our own thing instead."

"It's okay." Before I could say anything more, a familiar voice caught our attention.

"Hey, ladies!" Xavier greeted us with a grin. He was shirtless, showing off his incredible physique and olive skin. His blue swim trunks and wavy dark hair completed his entire beach vibe, and if he wasn't such a womanizer, I *might* have found him attractive…

But honestly, it was a no from the get-go with him.

I just didn't want Luke to know that. I liked making him sweat. It was literally the only thing I could do to attempt to block out the heartache.

"Where is everyone?" Xavier asked, plopping down on the edge of my chair. I moved my feet to keep from brushing up against him. I might flirt, but no touching.

"I don't know," Delilah answered, shrugging her shoulders and leaning back in her chair. "Jett is out on the yacht with Ronny, the mechanic. As far as the rest...no idea."

"Hmm...where's your, uh, ex?" Xavier turned his attention solely to me.

"I have no idea," I answered him in a nonchalant tone. "I'm not his keeper."

"He sure as hell thinks he's yours," Xavier chuckled, flipping some of his dark waves. "I swear the guy gives me all these threatening looks, like they're going to keep me away from you. He gives off bear vibes, you know? But I think he's all bark, no bite."

*You wouldn't think that if you'd seen the guys he's beaten up over me.*

"I don't know, but don't be starting any drama," Delilah warned, jumping in to cover me. "The goal of this trip is to just have a good time. I don't want to break up fistfights when I'm supposed to be relaxing."

He grinned. "I'd never let you break one of those pretty nails breaking up a fight. Xavier the Beast can handle himself."

I almost couldn't conceal my cringe. "What?"

He turned to me. "Yeah, didn't you know I almost went pro in MMA? I was nuts right after high school. You don't have to worry about your safety when I'm around."

"Right," I snorted.

"I'm serious," he said, laughing. "You all just don't remember because you were way too cool for me in high school."

"You didn't even know we existed," I shot back, shaking my head. "There were so many kids in our classes it was impossible to keep up with everyone."

"You make a good point," Xavier agreed. "Sometimes I wish I would've gone to a smaller school. When my ten-year reunion comes up, I won't know most of the people there."

I shrugged. "I didn't go to mine." I had purposefully dodged it just in case Luke showed up.

"You didn't miss anything," Delilah grumbled. "It was literally the *most* boring event I have ever been to. Jett and I left after like two hours."

I opened my mouth, almost asking if she had seen Luke there, but I held back. It didn't matter if he had or hadn't been—and I was pretty sure Delilah *might* have mentioned it if she had seen him.

"Ah, there's everyone!" Xavier jumped up to his feet, seeing a large group of people headed our way. He ran off to greet them all, but I stayed where I was, trying not to see if Luke was with them.

"I swear, why didn't we go off on our own trip?" Delilah muttered, eyeing the models jumping up and down in their tiny bikinis.

"I don't know, but you shouldn't be intimidated." I gave her a reassuring smile. "Your husband only has eyes for you. I've seen it over and over. He doesn't even look twice at any of them."

"Oh, no, I know," she laughed. "Though right now, I'm pretty sure he only has eyes for the yacht. Honestly, I was just hoping that this would be a *friend's* trip. I wasn't expecting him to invite the whole company."

I shrugged. "I'm not surprised."

"Yeah, he said they all deserved a break, and the yacht was big enough for all of them. He swore it would be more fun, but I find it annoying being in the presence of twenty-one-year-olds who spend more time taking pics for their social media than actually enjoying the vacation."

"Meh, let them do whatever they want," I said with a shrug. "At least it gives us a chance to just relax and read for a while."

"You're just saying that because of Xavier." She eyed me, giving me a silly face. "But I hate to break it you, Layla, he might be...whatever he is...but I'm already catching on that he's loving the idea of the challenge you represent. Those girls will only keep his attention until Luke shows up—and then he'll be all over you."

I let out a sigh. *God, I hope not.*

# 8

## Luke

"So the boat is fixed?" I asked Jett as we trudged through the sand, weaving through the crowd of people.

"I mean, Ronny says it should be okay to take it out, just not to go too far. I guess it's right on the verge of needing to be scrapped in its entirety." Jett let out a burdened sigh. "Amazing how there's lemons everywhere, no matter how much money you spend."

"Yeah, you remember my first car," I chuckled, thinking back to the two-hundred-thousand-dollar sports car my dad had bought for me.

"You blew the motor on that car because you kept trying to race Malcom Hendrix." Jett gave me a side-eye. "I have done nothing but baby the fuck out of this boat, and it just keeps failing me."

"You sound like you're in a bad relationship, bro." I clapped my hand on his shoulder and squeezed. "Might be time to buy a replacement."

"Already looking," he grumbled. "I wish I would've done it before this. I have half of my damn company here."

"So just rent a yacht then?"

"No way, they don't want to be on a rental."

"Okay then, I guess just don't go out very far, and it'll all be good." I shrugged my shoulders, turning to gaze toward the volleyball net. There were a *ton* of people surrounding it, and I grimaced at the sight. It was clear the party had grown beyond just those Jett had invited.

"This is why I like the yacht," Jett muttered as we approached. He slapped a goofy smile on his face and greeted everyone, but I only searched for one person...

*Layla.*

I had been meaning to get out to the beach faster but had gotten wrapped up in pouring over the documents Jackson had sent me. The company was in great shape financially, so it wasn't *that* big of a risk to buy, but that still didn't mean I wanted to. Whether Jackson wanted to admit it or not, he wasn't exactly the best when it came to being a businessman. So, if I was truly a silent partner, that would leave it up to Eli to run, and he had enough on his plate with Whiss Productions.

"Well, look who finally decided to show up," Delilah said smoothly, looking up from the book she was reading. "How's our Laguna Girl?"

"She's a piece of shit," Jett grunted, plopping down in the empty chair beside her. "I think we might have to let her go."

Her face scrunched. "Can't we just redo her?"

"Whatever you wanna do, baby." Jett gave her a soft smile that made me want to vomit—well, mostly. There was also an indiscriminate pang of jealousy...

But I ignored that.

"You're *fire* at this!" Xavier's voice caught my attention, and I whipped my head in his direction.

And then my fucking mouth dropped open.

# LUKE

Layla was out there in the middle of the game, her dark hair pulled up in a bun on her head and her body clad in a olive-colored bikini...

*Fuck me.*

It was high-cut in the back, giving the whole beach a view at just how peachy her ass was, and the front *hardly* held in her ample tits. Her aviators glinted under the Florida sun, and her creamy skin had a hint of a tan—but I still hoped she'd put on sunscreen...

And that Xavier hadn't offered a hand.

"I was terrible at sports in school," Layla said to him, shrugging her shoulders. "I think I've just been lucky today."

"Hardly luck the way you hit the ball. Don't be humble. You're a badass, Layla. I'm fuckin' smitten."

*I'll fuckin' smite you, bro.*

"You're too sweet," Layla giggled, dismissing him with a wave.

My nerves were shot within seconds of hearing her react like that. She didn't even know I was here, so there was no way it was just her trying to make me jealous—and that was stupid of me to assume anyway.

"Hey, Luke." Xavier looked over at me while Layla looked out across the ocean. "Why don't you play?"

"I don't play sports."

"With a body like that, I bet you do," he shot back at me.

"Nope. Just lift a lot of weights and run."

Layla finally looked over at me, the smile on her face fading to a frown for a moment. "Just let him be."

*Oof.* That fucking burned.

But I clenched my jaw instead of throwing back an insult. I wasn't in the mood to play volleyball with all the people who had congregated here. I grabbed a lounge chair and tucked it next to Jett and Delilah, hoping they would serve as a distraction...

But it was fucking *impossible* not to watch Layla's ass bounce as she moved. She *was* athletic, whether she wanted to admit it or not. She made it look easy, carrying most of the weight for her team...

And it was *hot.*

"Damn, I never knew she had that kind of skill," Delilah laughed, setting her book down in her lap. "She always told me she had no athleticism."

"She clearly picked that up *after* high school," Jett said, a smirk growing on his face. "Because she was awkward as hell back then. I don't think she could walk on flat ground without tripping over herself."

I smiled, thinking back to the Layla I'd fallen in love with. "She was pretty clumsy, but I don't know...it was endearing."

Both of them looked over at me, their eyes wide.

"What?"

"I think that might be the first time he's smiled since he showed up here," Jett cackled as he popped open a beer from the ice chest.

"He's not wrong, you know," Delilah agreed, eyeing me. I had only met her a handful of times, since by the time they'd met, Jett and I lived a thousand miles away. She was nice from what I could tell, though I had to admit that I automatically held the fact that Layla was her best friend against her.

"Can I have one of those?" I gestured to the ice chest next to Jett.

He handed me the one he'd just opened and grabbed another for himself. "So, I'm thinking we should take the yacht out this evening. It's supposed to be a clear night, and it's gotta be better than this shit." He motioned toward all of the random people who had gathered around us. "I don't like the crowd."

"Then why did you decide on a resort *right* in the middle of one of the biggest tourist cities on the gulf coast?" I leveled with him, letting out a chuckle. "You should've just taken us to Deb's island."

"I don't think Deb would've let us." He let out a sigh, rolling his eyes at the mention of his rich-ass cousin. "She doesn't let anyone do anything out there. She spent millions of dollars on some dumbass island that *no one* ever visits—not even her."

"Yeah, but that's because it's literally in the middle of the Indian Ocean."

"And boats disappear around it," Delilah threw out, visibly shuddering. "I don't know why she doesn't just sell it and cut her losses at this point."

My eyes flickered away from the conversation and back to Layla, still bouncing around in the sand next to Xavier. He was all smiles, playfully giving her a high five while his hand lingered against hers. She glanced over in our direction before pulling away, and even through her aviators...

I knew she was looking at me.

This was some sort of *fuck you* that just wasn't sitting right—at all. The jealousy was an unwelcome emotion that I hadn't experienced in so long. No woman had ever evoked these kinds of feelings from me.

Well, except for Layla.

"Quit staring." Jett kicked me, his foot landing right in the center of my calf. "We all know you have a hard-on for Layla, but you're embarrassing yourself. Just let her be."

"Fuck off," I grunted, shooting him a glare. "I'm not staring."

"Well, if you're not drooling over Layla, you're shooting daggers at Xavier. You look like you're out for blood." Jett laughed, and Delilah rolled her eyes.

"I don't know why men are so ridiculous."

"Because we think with our dicks and not our brains half the time." Jett grimaced, shooting her a wink. "But my dick only thinks about you, so you don't have to worry about anything."

"Good to know. Otherwise, I might have to cut it off."

"I love it when you talk dirty to me." He wiggled his eyebrows before squeezing her upper thigh. "You wanna just head back to the room?"

"Sure, I think I brought my pocketknife." She stuck out her tongue at him, and I chuckled, while Jett went in for a kiss.

*To have something like that...*

Well, minus the whole cutting a dick off thing. I could go without that kind of foreplay. My gaze drifted back out to the volleyball game, but Layla and Xavier must've rotated out, both of them heading right for us.

"Good game," Xavier commented before plopping down in the sand by the ice chest. "You really missed out, Luke." The smirk on his face annoyed me, but as much as I wanted to punch his lights out, I was just gonna let him think he won...

For now, anyway.

"So, the yacht is fixed?" Layla asked, her eyes focused on Jett as she took a seat on a beach towel under the shade of the umbrellas. She slid her aviators up to rest on her head and leaned back on her hands.

"Yeah, I guess you could say that," Jett muttered. "I was thinking we would take it out this evening. It'll be a nice change of pace from today."

"You don't like the crowd of beautiful women?" Xavier shot Jett a toothy grin. "I swear, there's no place like Miami beaches."

"Yeah..." Jett didn't return the smile. "Anyway, what do you guys think about it? I was thinking we could leave around eight."

Xavier shook his head. "I'll have to sit this one out. I have to be at one of my clubs tonight. There's a huge party going on for one of the club managers. Supposed to be a huge turnout. I have to go, but I think we all should."

*Uh, hell to the no.*

"Um…I'll probably skip on that," Delilah said, shrugging her shoulders. "I love a good night out, but this is a vacay that I'd like to take slow. We have to do enough of that kind of stuff for work."

"But half of your company is here," Xavier pointed out, his eyes going to Jett.

Jett pursed his lips. "Yeah, I get that, but I'm with my wife. I'm not in the mood to go clubbing."

"I'll go to the club with you," Layla offered, causing my mouth to drop open. I picked my jaw up quickly, noting the sly look on Delilah's face as the two of them made eye contact.

*Is she seriously going after Xavier?*

I had to swallow the frustration and whatever else I felt in the moment. I *knew* Xavier was nothing but trouble. I mean, sure, he was safe—but he couldn't keep Layla safe like I could.

"So we'll just give everyone the option," Xavier said, shooting Layla a smile. They either get on the yacht, or they come to my club with me."

"Sounds fair," Jett agreed, before turning to look at me. "What're you gonna be doing, Luke? You've been quiet this whole time."

Everyone's eyes focused on me, Layla's included. My jaw tensed at the question, because as much as I would rather just relax on the yacht…

There was no way I was letting Xavier get his hands on Layla.

# 9

# Layla

I only agreed to go to the club because the thought of being stuck on the yacht with Luke tonight just didn't sound appealing. I knew that since it was fixed, we'd all be going out on it nearly every day, so when there was an option to avoid Luke altogether...I was going to take it. However, going to the club did mean spending more time with Xavier, and I had been practicing my flirt game...

Maybe a little too much.

"What do you want to drink?" Xavier asked, returning to where I was sitting at the club bar. He waved down one of the very busy bartenders before I could even answer.

"What can I get for you?" The bartender was a hot blonde who for some reason reminded me of Paris Hilton, though I couldn't put my finger on why.

"Um...I'll just have a sex on the beach?"

"Yeah, just like everyone else," she muttered, spinning around and heading off to make my drink.

"Don't mind Cely," Xavier chuckled, his eyes transfixed on me. "She's always in a bad mood. She's the kind of woman with a chip on her shoulder, but too hot to turn away from the job. She draws them in."

I nodded, completely unamused by his reasoning. "I see. Well, I suppose it's whatever works best for you."

"You might work best for me." He smirked, running his hand down my arm. "And I was thinking we could go upstairs to the more private area? The lounge is a lot less demanding. Out here, even in the VIP, you can hardly have a conversation."

As much as I did *not* want to be alone with Xavier, I also was on the verge of a bad fucking headache. "Okay. That actually sounds nice."

"Perfect."

Cely, the bartender with the chip on her shoulder, brought me my drink. "Here, hope you enjoy that."

Before I could even say thanks, she had turned around and headed off to another customer. Xavier nodded for me to follow him to a set of stairs that led to a balcony, and I pushed off the edge of the bar. His club was nice—one of the nicest I had ever been to—but I just didn't go out often since having Autumn. And when I did, I preferred low-key dive bars.

My red strappy heels pushed the limits of my balance as I followed Xavier up the spiral staircase. I had worn a tight black dress with a crisscross front, leading to a *lot* of side boob for the world to enjoy. It was definitely out of my comfort zone…

But so was playing volleyball in a bikini.

I smiled to myself at the memory, the shocked expression on Luke's face coming to mind. I had seen him coming way off down the beach and had promptly dropped my cover-up before he made it there. I'd thought his eyes might pop out of his head.

"So, you live in LA?" Xavier asked as soon as we made it to the second floor. It was darker up here, and the small stripper stage in the middle of a bunch of designer furniture left me wondering just how comfortable it really was. A woman in tassels and a black thong was working the pole, while a few men and women sat around taking.

"Uh...I used to, but most of my family is in NYC, and now I live outside of Miami." I choked out the words when I noticed Xavier staring at me, waiting for my answer. "It's nice there," I added stupidly, hardly able to take my eyes off the fit woman working the pole.

"That's Gabby." Xavier gestured to the woman with a smile. "She's got mad pole-dancing skills and my associates prefer to keep her up here most nights. They tip better and she doesn't have to deal with the creeps at strip clubs." He made it sound honorable, so I only nodded, biting back the question of what else Gabby had to do up here.

Xavier plopped down on one of the couches positioned to the right of the stage, and then patted the seat beside him, looking up at me. "I don't bite. At least, not yet."

I forced a smile as I sat down next to him. I ensured there were a solid few inches between the two of us, though he threw his arm around the back of the couch before I'd even gotten settled. My heart picked up its pace—but not with excitement—just pure apprehension.

*I should've just gone out on the yacht.*

But in an attempt to avoid Luke, I was just making myself miserable. I missed my best friend and lying out under the stars. Instead, I was stuck watching Gabby work the pole while I sipped on a college-level drink. It was *not* my forte.

"So...what's up with Luke? Obviously, I know the two of you have history, but the tension between the two of you screams more than just a decade ago."

I whipped my head around. "Uh...I don't know. There's nothing going on between us." I didn't know why the question caught me off guard, but I was already feeling myself growing defensive.

Xavier chuckled, downing the rest of his drink. "That definitely means something is going on. I know how women are about their exes. Luke Whiss is a billionaire, and no matter how much we all want to play him off as an asshole, he's an asshole with a *lot* of money. I don't know a woman who wouldn't be all over that."

I shook my head, disgust filling my chest. "I *never* go after a guy because of his money."

"Right, okay." Xavier burst into a fit of laughter. "I can't count the times a woman has said that to me, and then asked for my credit card a few weeks later."

*Oof, he's been burned.*

"Well, that's not my style." There was no point in acting offended, because obviously the guy had reservations about it.

"Okay, okay." His fingers brushed my bare shoulder, and I found myself slumping out of his reach. "So I know you and Luke dated through high school—but what happened after? Just broken hearts fueling the tension between the two of you?"

"I don't know." I cleared my throat before sipping on my drink. "I guess we just didn't end that great. It should be water under the bridge."

"But it's not," he pointed out. "Luke wants to fuckin' jump me over being around you. He's already threatened it."

*Of course he has.*

However, the thought of Luke *actually* making a threat to Xavier made my thighs clench. My body was betraying me—just like in the elevator.

"I'm not intimidated by the challenge," he continued when I didn't say anything. "I find men like Luke to be intriguing and almost exciting. There's nothing like stealing the woman they're trying to be possessive over. Just something about it turns me on."

I grimaced inwardly, growing more and more uncomfortable. "That's an interesting fact."

He leaned into my ear, his eyes drifting out to Gabby on the stage. "What turns you on, Layla?"

*Not you.*

*Not this.*

"Uh..." My voice trailed off, wishing there was some excuse I could come up with to get the fuck out of here. "I don't know." Reaching into my purse, I pulled my phone out, seeing a text from my sister.

*How's it going?*

"Is that important?" Xavier murmured, shifting his body closer to mine.

"Yeah, it is," I snapped, putting some space between us so I could text Lily back. This text was going to take a *long* time. However, I was only a few words in when Xavier called over my shoulder.

"Who the hell let you up here?"

I jerked my head around to see who he was talking to, and the moment my eyes met Luke's, I nearly fell apart with...*relief.*

"I asked where the party was, and they told me up here," Luke said in a flat tone. His lips turned down in a frown as he glanced at Gabby, shaking her ass on the stage. He shook his head and headed toward the two of us, a beer in his hand. "This is an interesting club you've got here."

"Yeah, not really your kind of place." Xavier narrowed his eyes as Luke plopped down right beside me on the couch.

# LAYLA

"Oh yeah, this is *definitely* not my kind of place," Luke grunted, his eyes everywhere *but* the stage in front of us. "I prefer to just hit the odd dive bar—if I go out at all."

"You sound like a loser," Xavier chuckled. "You got all that money, and you're not enjoying it in the slightest."

"I mean, everyone has their own thing," I said carefully, noticing the way both men stared at me. Xavier appeared annoyed by my response, while Luke chuckled.

"Why don't you show us what you've got?" Xavier gestured up to the pole as Gabby stepped off to give one of the men a lap dance. "I bet all that volleyball skill you have can translate to the pole. I know you have the body for it."

My eyes went wide, and I could swear Luke radiated a whole new level of heat. "I don't...I don't know anything about pole dancing."

"I think you should just do it," Xavier laughed. "It's just for fun, anyway. Women hop up there all the time to try it out. You're in a safe place."

"Would hardly call this safe," Luke grumbled beneath his breath.

"I don't think so," I said, ignoring Luke's comment. I glanced down to my hands and when I did, I realized I had scooted closer to Luke than Xavier, our bodies nearly touching.

*That's where the heat is coming from.*

My heart stuttered in my chest as I caught a whiff of his familiar cologne, and my pussy reacted, remembering what it felt like to have his head between my legs.

*Ugh.*

I got the courage to look up at the man sitting next to me, and as I did, my breath hitched. Luke's eyes were focused on me—not the lap dance taking place just across the room.

"You don't like it here," he said in a low, soft voice. "You don't have to stay."

I swallowed the need to agree, remembering that Luke had the power to destroy me. "It was fine until you showed up."

He rolled his eyes. "Don't do that."

"Do what?"

"Deflect everything. It's the truth, Layla, and you know it. This isn't your kind of place, and you're not fooling me."

Before I could give him a snarky reply, I felt the couch shift. I looked over, seeing Xavier pushing himself into a standing position. He didn't even look back at us as he made his way to Gabby, grabbing her hand and pulling her into his lap at the same time as he sat down on the other couch.

*Wow. Dick move.*

My mouth dropped open, and even though I wasn't into him, I was still a little put off by it. I wasn't jealous at all, just...*disgusted*.

"I told you, he's not the kind of guy you wanna be around." Luke's *I told you so* voice was annoying, but I understood now.

"I never wanted to be with him." I stood to my feet. Smoothing out my dress, I headed for the staircase. I had no qualms leaving both Xavier *and* Luke behind.

"I'll take you back to the resort," Luke offered, grabbing my hand to stop me at the bottom of the stairs. "I don't wanna be here either."

"Then *why* are you here, Luke?" I asked, exasperated, ripping my arm away from him.

His jaw tightened as his eyes met mine. "You know damn well why I'm here."

# 10

## Luke

Layla was dead silent the entire ride back to the resort. She sat on the opposite side of the backseat, her seat belt pulled tightly around her. I tried not to stare at her, but *fuck*, the way her tits were nearly falling out of her black dress...

Yeah, it was a challenge.

She outshined every single woman in that place, but that was the way she'd always been—and she had no idea. She never had. And as angry as I'd been about the way Xavier was flirting and touching her...

Her discomfort was much more concerning.

"Have a nice night, you two," the Uber driver said to us as he pulled up under the awning.

"You too," I grunted as Layla flung the door open, sliding out and stalking toward the front doors.

"Good luck with that," the driver chuckled, giving me a sympathetic smile.

I let out a sigh and hurried out, jogging to catch up with her as she stepped into the elevator. "What's wrong?" I demanded.

"*Nothing.*"

"Wow, that's *so* convincing, Layla," I grumbled, rolling my eyes as I punched the button for her floor. "You were clearly having a horrible time there, and I got you out—and you're *still* being rude as fuck to me."

She spun around to face me, the hue of gold in her eyes aglow with anger. "I could've handled myself. I would've easily called my own freaking Uber and gotten a ride back to the resort. I didn't need you to save me, so don't start with that hero complex you have. You're *not* my hero."

"You were sitting there, *letting* him touch you even though you looked miserable as hell—the dude had you watching a *stripper.* Who *does* that with someone they're interested in?"

"Oh, don't be such a saint, Luke," she spat at me as she stepped out onto her floor. "I'm sure if you weren't so *jealous,* you would've been enjoying the show too!"

Anger raged in my chest as I stalked after her down the hall. "I wasn't jealous! I was trying to protect you from that asshole. I told you he was bad news, Layla." I felt freaking desperate in the moment, chasing her down the hall. That's how it had been since high school—I'd chase her, and she'd leave me.

"Oh, don't even try to put on some front. I *know* you were jealous." She stopped just outside her door, having opened it just a crack. "You've always been the jealous kind. You don't want me, but no one else can have me either." Her eyes bore into mine and I couldn't catch my breath. I was *so* turned on by the way her hands were on her hips, and she had that *I might kill you or fuck you* look on her face.

"Xavier is a dick."

Layla's lips twitched like she might smile, but she didn't. "I know that."

I took a step closer to her, my hand landing on the doorframe. "So why're you fucking around with him?"

She audibly swallowed, her head tilting up to look at me. "I was just having fun."

"Or were you *trying* to make me jealous? Because you've been throwing that word out a lot."

"Fuck you, Luke," she nearly whispered, her eyes seething with anger.

"I dare you to."

She grabbed my white dress shirt, jerking my mouth to hers. I let out a groan the moment my lips tasted the remnants of a fruity drink on her tongue. Her kiss was full of rage, and it made my cock throb, constricted by my dark jeans.

We stumbled backward, the door slamming into the wall. I reached for it, slinging it back the opposite way to shut us in. I knew in my head this was a mistake—I knew what it would lead to—but ever since the elevator incident I'd had a set of blue balls...

And there was only one woman who would satisfy me.

"Get this off," Layla panted as she broke her lips from mine, ripping at the buttons of my shirt. I ripped it over my head to save time, throwing it somewhere across the room as I went for the hem of her dress.

In one big swooping motion, I took the thing right off, leaving her in nothing but a black satin thong.

*Oh fuck.*

Her tits were so full and so perky, her nipples erect and ready for my mouth. I went for her body, my lips sucking in the skin of her neck as my hands pored over every single inch of her body. It felt like a fucking *dream* to have her body against mine again.

And not in a stupid elevator.

Her fingers fumbled with the button on my jeans, ripping them open and tugging them down. My cock bounced free, and my breath hitched as her hand grabbed my shaft, pumping it eagerly—and angrily. I kicked off the rest of my clothes and carried her to the bed, tossing her onto the white duvet.

"You don't have to be so delicate with me," she challenged, biting her lip as I crawled onto the bed.

"You want it hard then? You know you're playing with fire," I growled, grabbing her ankles and forcing her onto her stomach. I knew how to have angry sex. And I knew how Layla liked it.

I slipped my arm under her body, bringing her ass up into the air. My finger slipped between her ass cheeks, running between her slick, wet folds.

"You're always wet for me, aren't you?" I panted, just before shoving two fingers inside of her tight pussy.

She let out a cry in response, her legs trembling with want. Whatever the fuck had happened between us must've gotten her going, and I was going to fuck her until she couldn't remember any other man but me. I pumped my fingers in and out of her a few times, and she ground against me in response, her ass bouncing.

Removing my fingers, I salivated at the way they glistened from her moisture. I slapped her ass and shoved them into my mouth, cleaning them up as Layla whimpered. I glanced down at her, meeting her pretty green eyes—and gave her a wicked smile.

"Wouldn't you love for my tongue to be inside of you," I teased her, leaning over and kissing her ass. "Maybe I should leave you cold the way you did me."

She glared at me. "Or maybe you should just fuck me instead of sitting there playing with your fingers."

I smiled at the dare and grabbed her hips roughly. I let out a possessive growl as I forced my thick cock deep inside of her.

"*Oh, fuck!*" Layla cried out, as I filled every inch of her tight pussy. I slapped her ass again and then put an iron grip around her waist, holding her while I slammed into the back of her.

"You *were* jealous," she taunted me in between cries, and I knew she was purposefully trying to piss me off. We used to have some incredible makeup sex.

"You were trying to *make* me jealous," I growled back at her, popping her ass again. "And this is what you fucking get."

She whined in response, and I grabbed her hair, fisting it in my hands for leverage. Layla's head tipped back, and the pleasure written all over her face made my dick throb with satisfaction. She wanted this.

"*Ooh...*" she purred through her thick, swollen lips as her eyes closed.

Yeah, she couldn't even think about smarting off to me now. I tugged a little harder, fucking her with all the force I had in me. Her tits bounced beneath her, and as I watched them, I realized I wanted a better view.

Releasing her hair, I pulled out of her and flipped her over, loving the surprise on her face as I did so. I worked my way up her body, positioning my wet dick right in between her tits.

"Put those tits on me," I ordered.

Layla seductively grinned as she pressed her breasts together, squeezing my dick. "Like this?"

"*Fuck,*" I groaned out as she bounced them up and down my shaft. She was the only woman I had ever let do this to me, and it got me every single fucking time. I began to thrust between them, my tip nearly touching her chin. "I love your tits."

"You always have," she teased, bouncing them faster. Her soft, creamy skin looked like porcelain against my tan complexion and her breasts were flawless—just like her entire body. She bit her lip, holding my gaze with a seductive glimmer in her eyes, and I fought the urge to just explode all over her...

But I wasn't done.

I pulled my dick out from between her perfect breasts, before leaning down and sucking one of her nipples into my mouth. I tasted a hint of her pussy there, and I grunted with the satisfaction of my two favorite things in one place. I took my sweet time, going between both of them before burying my face in her chest.

And then I flipped us over.

She squealed at the swift motion, planting her body on top of me. "*Luke!*"

"Get on my fucking face," I growled, slapping her ass as she sat up. She dragged her wet pussy up my chest, and anticipation got the best of me. I lifted her up, setting her right on my mouth.

"Oh my *god*," she whimpered as my tongue teased her from below. Layla gripped the headboard, shifting herself until her pussy was hovering just above me. I grabbed her, not satisfied with the distance.

I wanted her pussy *suffocating* me.

Layla cried out as I sat her tightly against me. My hands rested on her ass, but I didn't hold her too tight, giving her the freedom to move. She understood the assignment and immediately began to ride my face like the dirty girl she was.

Her pussy filled my mouth with her sweet juices, quenching a thirst I'd felt ever since the elevator. I drank like she was booze and I was an alcoholic, determined to get my fill. Her moaning filled the room, and I hoped the entire place heard her crying out my name.

Especially Xavier.

My tongue covered every inch of her center, and as submissive as it felt to have her on my face, the satisfaction was worth it. She rode me faster and harder as she edged near climax. I slapped her ass as she ground her pussy all over me.

"I'm gonna cum," she whined, more moisture lathering my tongue. "Oh, oh, *Luke*!" She let out a scream as her pussy exploded, pulsing around my tongue and covering me with all of her. I grabbed her waist then, holding her against me as I licked her clean.

She panted as she came down from the high, and after I was sure I had covered every crevice and square inch of her skin, I shifted her off my face. Her eyes were glowing, though her face was hazy with lust.

And suddenly, my fucking feelings betrayed me. My heart did a flip-flop in my chest, and we stared at each other for a few long seconds while she sat on my chest, looking down at me.

*It's just a fuck.*

I broke our locked gaze as I reminded myself that this was nothing to me. I rolled her off of me and onto her back. Grabbing her legs, I rested an ankle against each of my shoulders.

And then I pulled her tight little pussy right onto my cock. She bit down on her lip as her tits bounced all over the place, giving me just the view I needed to finish...

Because I damn sure wasn't going to be looking into those emerald eyes.

I fucked her harder than ever, her face contorted from the force as she let out little cries. I didn't slow down or let up because I was fucking *angry* all over again. She brought out *all* the feelings that I thought I had forgotten. I thought I had moved on.

*I just want to fuck her. No feelings.*

But as my body drew tense for my climax, my heart kept haphazardly stuttering in my chest with emotion. My iron grip dug into her hips as I held her in place.

"*Luke,*" she moaned. "*Oh. My. God. Luke.*"

I wanted to yell at her to stop saying my name like that. It reminded me of all the times she had whispered she loved me in my ear.

And I couldn't stand it...

Except that was the biggest lie I could tell myself. I fucking *loved* it, and as she said my name one last time, I pulled out...

And blew my load all over those perfectly perky tits of hers.

*Fuck me.*

She let out a cute sigh as I climbed off the bed, heading to the bathroom. My head was a wreck, but I wasn't going to run off and leave her on the bed covered in my cum. I grabbed a hand towel from the stack and dampened it with warm water.

"I can do that myself," she snapped at me as I reappeared from the bathroom. "I don't need you to clean me up."

I ignored her complaints, leaning over her and gently wiping away the mess I had made. Her breath hitched as I cleaned around her nipples, the pink tips still erect. My dick threatened to come back alive, but I pushed the thought away. Layla would more than likely just ask me to go.

"Thanks," she muttered, sitting up as soon as I finished. "You're the only guy who's ever done anything like that."

Irritation leapt in my chest at the thought of any other man touching her. "You must really go after gentlemen then."

"Well, if I have bad taste, maybe you should take a look in the mirror," she snorted, grabbing up an oversized T-shirt from one of the dresser drawers.

"Touché," I chuckled, ending the sparring. I pulled on my boxer briefs and headed back to the bed beside her, plopping down and laying my head on the pillow. She looked over at me wearily.

"I don't hate you," she said, her lids suddenly looking heavy as she rolled onto her side to face me.

"Thanks for the information, Layla." My tone was soft and playful, and honestly, it *was* a win that she didn't hate me...but it didn't satisfy something deep inside of me—the same part of me that felt all those feels in the middle of sex...

The part of me that was still in love with her.

# 11

# *Layla*

*Oh my god, he's still here.*

I rolled over in bed, the sound of Luke's snoring arousing me from my sleep. *How much did I have to drink last night? How much did he have?* I wasn't sure about the second question, but I knew I hadn't drunk enough to do anything more than just take the edge off...

My mind filled with the images of our rowdy sex—as embarrassing as it was, I had fallen asleep as soon as he'd crawled back into bed—and all I could remember telling Luke after sex was that I didn't hate him...

*Ugh.*

I only wished that I could. My heart hammered in my chest as he drew in long, steady, calm breaths. Apprehension was creeping into my body. What was I supposed to say to him when he woke up? Should I tell him about Autumn? Did he even know that I had a kid? My unruly thoughts drove me out of bed, and I grabbed my phone as I headed toward the balcony. I swung the door open and stepped outside.

# LAYLA

It was early, and the warm glow of the sunrise was stunning enough to distract me for a few moments. Had this kind of night happened ten years ago in a place like this, I would've thought I was in heaven...

But now it rivaled hell.

I had to protect my heart from the man who broke it, and being underneath—or on top—of him was not doing myself any favors. I needed to get my head on straight, and there was one person I knew would root me back into reality.

"Why are you calling me at six-thirty in the morning?" my sister groaned, her voice still groggy with sleep. "The girls literally *just* got up, and I haven't had coffee yet."

"Perfect," I said. "I need the crabbiest version of you."

"Oh god, what did you do?" Lily muttered, and I knew she was shaking her head at me on the other end of the phone. "I swear if this has something to do with Luke..."

"He's asleep in my bed right now."

"You have to be kidding me. Didn't we *just* have a conversation about how you should *not* be getting involved with him? You're supposed to be having fun, not screwing your ex-boyfriend and secret baby daddy."

*Ah, just what I need to hear.*

"It was kind of fun though," I admitted, ready for the full-on verbal lashing.

"There is nothing fun about getting involved with that asshole. He's never done anything but break your heart—and you know that."

"I left last time," I pointed out, giving her all my doubts so that I could be set straight. "And he did get me out of an uncomfortable situation last night. I went to the club with Xavier and it was *not* what I wanted it to be."

"So you could've just Ubered yourself home," she snapped, and then let out a sigh. "You really should've waited to call until I had some coffee. You know how I am in the morning."

I grinned, plopping down in one of the soft chairs. "And *that* is why I called you. I don't know why he gets under my skin the way he does. The sex has always been so...*good*." My cheeks flushed as my thighs clenched, my body betraying me. If it were up to the cat between my legs, I'd be underneath Luke again right this second.

"Good sex is nothing in the big scheme of things," Lily said with a yawn. "If we're being honest, sex can be practiced until it's better as long as two people are willing to work at it."

"You must be speaking from experience," I teased.

"Shut it," she warned me, her voice still groggy. I heard the coffee maker on the other end of the phone, whirring to life. "But yeah, there might be some personal truth in there. Anyway, I just don't want to see you fall back into the vicious cycle with Luke. I watched you reel back in high school. He hid *everything* about you from his family."

The sting of the past threatened to slip up on me, but I pushed it away. "We're grown adults now though, and I think I could deal with just hooking up while we're on vacay."

She groaned, and I smiled at the thought of her facepalming. "No, Layla. Just...no. You're playing with fire—and you know that. What if he finds out about Autumn? We have worked *so* freaking hard to keep all that under wraps. Luke is a powerful, wealthy man. If he finds out about that secret, he might take you for all you're worth...and you could lose her."

My stomach knotted up at the thought. "You don't think he would actually do that, do you?"

"Well, did you think he would leave you scorned the way he did after high school? Our family was never good enough for his, and I don't want that to be amplified to Autumn."

I let out a sigh. Lily was just repeating the things I had shared with her, and as much as I'd wanted the conversation to be convincing, it wasn't totally working now that the subject had shifted to Autumn.

"Do you think I made a mistake not telling him?" I asked in a low voice, my gaze darting back to ensure that Luke was still sleeping soundly in my bed.

"Um...well...I think it's a little too late for this discussion, Layla." Lily let out a light laugh, her cranky attitude slipping away. "And quite frankly, I don't think you'd be second-guessing yourself if you hadn't brought the guy back into your bed. You acted like you hated him the last time we spoke, and now..."

"I've never *hated* him," I felt the need to clarify. "I'm not that kind of person. I just feel so many things right now, and I wonder if it would be different if he knew..."

"Of course it would be different," Lily said, sighing. "But I don't know how different it would be. If you think he would've magically changed his mind and asked you to marry him or something, I think you're wrong."

I nodded, squeezing my eyes shut for a long moment. "It's just like all the feelings I had for him never really went away. They're all right there under the surface."

"That's because you let him stick his dick in you," Lily's chiding voice returned. "He's an ex for a reason, let him be in the past. Besides, based on everything you've told me, I don't get the idea that he's up and changed. He seems like he's the same jealous guy he's always been. He probably just didn't want to see you with anyone else on the trip."

My chest felt tight at the thought. Maybe *that* was the only reason he had pursued me last night. After all, the whole thing had started over jealousy. *Ugh*. So toxic.

"Okay, well, I guess that settles that then," I grumbled, working out the tangles in my hair with my fingers. "I need to stop this before it gets the best of me."

"Probably a good idea," Lily said, before I heard a little voice in the background. "Your daughter knows that you're talking to me on the phone..."

I smiled. "You can put her on."

"Mommy!" Autumn cheered, her voice bright and clear—unlike Lily's. I imagined her bouncing up and down in my sister's kitchen, her messy hair bouncing on her shoulders.

"Good morning, Autumn," I greeted her, laughing. "How'd you sleep last night?"

"Um, I slept good, I guess," she answered me, her voice loud in my ear. "I had a dream that I was a princess and then I turned into a mermaid and then there was dolphins. Have you seen any dolphins?"

"That sounds like a great dream," I said, realizing just how much I missed her. "I haven't seen any dolphins yet, but I'll make sure I take pictures if I do so I can show you."

"Can you just bring one home?"

"No, I don't think that would be a good idea," I laughed, shaking my head. I loved the way kids always seemed to think the impossible was possible. "I might be able to find you a stuffed dolphin though."

"I already have a million of those," she sighed. "Aunt Lily said we can go to the aquarium today though. She said they might have dolphins there."

"Well, I'm not sure if they do or not, but that's nice of Aunt Lily to take you." I was almost positive there were no dolphins at the aquarium near my sister's house, but I'd let Lily work that one out.

"I need to eat my breakfast now," Autumn said, her voice growing distant. "Love you, Mommy!"

"Love you too, baby."

# 12

# Luke

*Love you too, baby?*

Who the hell was she talking to? My head was spinning from the words I swore I had heard, and I'd been awake for less than five minutes. I wanted to argue with myself and say I had just been dreaming, but I *knew* that was not out of my dreams.

Not the conscious kind, anyway.

*I need to get out of here.*

I sat up in the bed just as Layla appeared from the balcony, her phone in one hand and the other running her fingers through her wildly disheveled hair. No matter what the fuck she had said out there, she was gorgeous in her natural state, and I fought the urge to bring her right back to bed.

*But there's someone else...*

And the phone in her hand was the proof that I'd heard what I thought I had. Layla wasn't the type to two-time anyone—well, not the Layla that I knew...

"What were you doing?" I asked, trying not to sound as dejected as I felt.

Her face flashed with concern. "I was just on the phone with my sister."

I nodded, pursing my lips as she teetered back and forth. "So you call your sister *baby*?" I laughed sarcastically as I slid out of bed, going for my clothes. "That's not believable in the slightest."

Her eyes widened like a deer caught in headlights, but she didn't back down, her tone growing sharp and defensive. "I have a niece, Luke."

"Right," I quipped, shaking my head as I continued to pull on my clothes. "You can say whatever you want."

"Are you seriously trying to say that I would *cheat* on someone?" The anger in her tone suddenly shifted to wounded, and I looked back up her, seeing the storm in her eyes. "Why would you even sleep with me if that's really what you think of my character?"

I bit the inside of my cheek, knowing I had jumped too fast—but my pride reminded me of the break she'd given me years ago. "I don't really know you anymore," I said, ensuring my wallet and room key were still in my pocket. "And I heard what I heard."

She threw up her hands, growing more and more wound up by the minute. "What *did* you even hear?"

"Enough," I snapped, spinning on my heel and heading toward the exit.

"Stop." Her fingers wrapped around my wrist. "I wasn't talking to a guy on the phone, I swear."

I spun around and pulled away from her, taking in her expression. She was difficult to read in the moment, but there was a sense of panic in her voice that I couldn't decipher. Why did she even care what I thought? She'd run out on me the last time we did anything. Besides, this was just a hookup...right?

Before I let my mouth move and spill out anything I might regret, I turned back toward the door. "This can't happen again," I snapped, ripping it open and stepping out into the hallway. She said something incoherent in response, but I didn't stop to listen to it. I needed to clear my head.

And get her out of it.

"Whoa, bud..."

*Fucking caught red-handed.*

"What's up, Jett?" I forced a smile as my best friend folded his arms across his chest in my direction.

"You know, really, that's a question I'd like to ask you. Last I checked, your room was on the second floor."

"Yeah, funny how easy it is to get turned around in a place like this," I snorted, rolling my eyes. I wasn't in the mood for jokes, not when my head was reeling after a night with Layla. I hated the way she made me feel *things*—things I never wanted to feel again—and yet, I couldn't resist the siren of a woman.

"Why don't you walk with me?" Jett suggested, cupping my shoulder with one of his extra-large hands as we headed for the elevator. "I think we should have a chat about what you were doing in Layla's room."

"I don't need to have a fuckin' chat about it."

"I really think we should." Jett reached past me and punched the down button for the elevator, letting out one of his *I'm about to lecture you* sighs. "I can make an assumption about what happened last night."

"Well, you know what they say about assumptions…" I eyed him as I stepped into the elevator. "Also, I don't need you to parent me. I have a dad for that."

"Dude." Jett shook his head. "Just stop. We both know you slept with Layla last night. There's no way you were just stopping in for an early morning conversation."

"You could maybe call it that," I joked, rubbing the stubble beginning to form on my jaw. However, I could tell Jett meant business based on the way his lips were in a straight line and eyes were devoid of any amusement.

"I thought you were over her," he said in flat voice. "In fact, I *banked* on the fact that you were over her. We're *best* friends, and you've been telling me you were over her since that shit happened in NYC *years* ago. Now, you're slipping out of her room at seven in the morning—well, sort of slipping out. That door slam was loud enough to wake the dead."

I grimaced, fighting off the embarrassment mixed with my wounded pride. "I was—well, *am*—over her," I said, though I was suddenly very unconvinced of it. "I don't know, I thought I was. But I swear, she sucks the oxygen right out of the room every time I see her. I also had no clue she was gonna be here." I shot him a glare. "Otherwise, I would've prepared."

"Well, in my defense, I had no idea you were actually coming until the day before you got here. Also…" He paused like he was searching for an excuse. "Okay, yeah, it's my bad. I should've told you she was coming. Honestly, I'm so used to you being far removed from my life. We only ever just talk on the phone, and I get that you live a busy life or whatever, but I don't know…"

I stepped off the elevator behind him, heading toward the breakfast bar. "It's fine. I haven't been that great of a friend these last few years," I admitted, guilt replacing all the mixed emotions I felt about Layla. Jett was my best friend, and while my work life was extremely successful, everything else was a fucking wreck.

And had been for years.

"It's all good. I get that you're busy with all those businesses, but..." His voice trailed off as he looked over to me. "You can make it up to me by telling me what the hell is going on with you and Layla. I know she's gonna spill the tea to my wife, so I better be in the loop. Because trust me, I am *never* in the loop when it comes to those two."

I let out a sigh as we were led toward a table in the back of the breakfast café. "I have a feeling there's nothing pleasant said about me. Delilah probably hates me...just like Layla does."

Jett laughed, shaking his head as he plopped down into the chair. "Women are way more complicated than you think. Any time Del has ever acted like she hated me, it was because I had done something that hurt her feelings."

"That's not even the same thing," I grunted, reaching for the water the waiter set down in front of me. "She *acts* like she hates you because she's mad or hurt—not because she actually does. I swear, Layla really does hate me."

"Well, it's not like you're some kind gentleman to her either," Jett countered, his tone chiding. "I don't exactly think you're some knight in shining armor. Let's not forget that you *hid* your entire relationship with her from your parents."

"That was high school," I snapped, shaking my head. "And you know how hard they were on my ass about not getting tied down until I had a career. And it was before Mom walked out; you know how weird she was about family standards."

"Excuse my language, but she was a bitch is what she was."

I chuckled, though it still stung thinking about her. The woman was my mother, but she wasn't even in my life anymore, living with some guy I had never met. "I don't want to talk about her, but yeah, I figured all that was water under the bridge when Layla and I rekindled shit in NYC."

Jett's face contorted with clear confusion. "Rekindled things how? Because I have never considered a one-night stand to be rekindling *anything*."

"It could've been more than a one-night stand had Layla not just taken off before I ever even woke up." Rejection still stung my words as I said them, and for the first time in years, I didn't hide it from Jett. "I don't know why she took off like that. We clicked just like we always had that night, and I thought there was a chance..."

His lips turned downward. "Did you tell her that?"

"Well, no." I shook my head. "I figured we would talk about it over coffee or something the next morning. We had spent the entire night just catching up on life, and then you can probably guess what filled the rest of the time."

"Yeah, spare the details." He chuckled, though it was flat. "But when we talked about it, you made it out like you just fucked and that was it."

I shrugged, feeling like I was in therapy—not breakfast. "I don't know, man, I didn't want to admit how bad it sucked that I woke up and she was gone."

"She probably felt the same way when you dumped her at the end of summer after senior year." There wasn't an ounce of sympathy in his voice as he picked up the water with his tattooed hand, his eyes challenging me. "I know for a fact that you destroyed her when you did that—I was there for the aftermath, and you weren't."

Anger crept into my chest. "Please tell me how you were there for my ex-girlfriend, Jett. Because we didn't talk for a whole fucking year after that."

"Because *you* chose to cut me off," he shot back, his volume taking a plunge. "You decided that you were just going to forget everyone, so while I went off to LA to go to college with Layla—like we *all* planned—you were suddenly at Harvard, doing what your mommy and daddy wanted."

I bit back the need to defend myself, hating that I'd caved to the pressure my now-absent mother had put on me. "I'm sorry," I forced out. "I thought we were past that."

He shook his head. "We *are* past that, Luke. I forgave you for that as soon as it happened. I know that your family life was complicated, but I'm just saying, you can't expect that same reaction from a woman who thought you were the love of her life. She let you hide *everything* and loved you unconditionally—and then you broke her heart."

"That was ten years ago," I muttered, though suddenly it was feeling like yesterday. "I don't know what I'm supposed to do now." My eyes met Jett's gaze, and for a split second, there was sympathy. "She was on the phone this morning, and she called whoever it was *baby*."

Jett nearly choked on his water as he set the glass back down on the table. "That's wild..."

I narrowed my eyes at him as his whole demeanor took a shift. "She told me it was her *niece*."

He nodded, his eyes shifting to the napkin on the table. "Yeah, she's close to her sister and her sister's daughter, Kody."

"At first I didn't believe her," I continued, wondering what the hell was making Jett act strange all of the sudden. "I thought it was a guy."

He burst into laughter, relaxing as he met my gaze. "Now *that* is definitely not something you have to worry about. The only thing close to a boyfriend Layla has is my wife."

I nodded, ignoring the nagging feeling that something was off. "Good to know. I guess maybe I should apologize to her about my assumption."

*Or maybe just leave her alone.*

But I knew as much as I wanted to believe I could do that...

It probably wasn't going to happen.

# 13

# Layla

*That was too close.*

I took a deep breath as I pulled on my bathing suit bottoms after taking a long, hot shower. Yeah, it was counterproductive to take a shower before heading out to get sand in all the places Luke had been last night, but...

I needed to wash him off me.

Lily was right about one thing, and that was the fact that I was putting Autumn at risk of being found out by messing around with Luke. I shook my head as I threw on my cover-up, my head a wreck of past and present emotions colliding. Frustratingly enough, I struggled to resist Luke, and the biggest wish I had...

Was that I didn't have to.

*Ugh.*

"Layla!" Delilah's voice was muffled as she pounded on the adjoining door. "Open this up. I know you're in there."

# LAYLA

I laughed, unlocking the deadbolt and opening the door to my best friend's curious face. "So nice of you to join me this morning."

"Mm-hmm." She gave me a sly smile. "And would you like to explain why I heard my husband run into Luke leaving your room this morning?"

My smile faded. I should've known. "Yeah, he showed up to the club last night—which strangely, I'm thankful for, because things got a little weird with Xavier... I don't think I'll be hanging out with him anymore. He's apparently into strippers."

She nodded, stepping into my room and taking a look around. "I have to say that I'm *not* surprised about Xavier. Jett has always said he's a little sleazy, but...Luke?" She turned to me with an eyebrow raised. "What's going on with that? You two act like you hate each other, but here you are..."

"Well, I doubt it'll be going anywhere now," I said, taking a seat on the edge of the bed. "I don't know what I was thinking getting involved with him. I just...things get *so* hot and heavy between us. It's like we go from zero to a hundred in a few tense seconds." My head dropped to my hands as I let out a frustrated groan. "And it doesn't help that I called my sister this morning to get a little reality dose—and he heard me tell Autumn I love her."

"So?" Delilah seemed confused as she took a seat beside me. "I don't understand why that would matter? I mean, I tell my sister I love her all the time."

"I said *baby*," I groaned, my best friend's eyes immediately widening. "And he obviously thought I was talking to a guy—because that makes total sense."

"Okay." She blew out a sharp breath. "And why can't he know you have a daughter? I mean, I get that it's some kind of big secret...but does Jett know that it's supposed to be a secret?"

My eyes went wide as I looked over to her. "I don't know. For all I know Luke *does* know that I have a daughter, actually."

Delilah laughed, and I had no idea how she found my clusterfuck of a life so funny. "Jett knows it's a secret."

"What?" My mouth dropped open. "How does he know?"

"Well, I thought he was oblivious to everything—that's what I told you, anyway. But I think he knows that Autumn is Luke's daughter...*and* that you're keeping it a secret. Maybe he just did the math, but he's definitely protecting your choice."

"Did you...*talk* to him about it?" My heart was hammering away in my chest, only imagining how terrible this could all go. But then again, if Jett had known all along, maybe that was better. He would've spilled it before now if he wanted to.

"He's my husband," Delilah said with a sigh. "I didn't bring it up last night though. He did. He wanted to know what I knew about you and Luke's past. He told me his suspicions—and I didn't *verbally* confirm them."

I rolled my eyes. "He just reads you like a book."

"Yeah, pretty much. I think he's on your side though—or he at least thinks it's your business. He's not getting involved."

"Good to know," I muttered, glancing down at my hands. This whole thing was going to blow up in my face if I didn't keep Luke separate from it...

Though I was quickly beginning to realize he had never been that far away.

"What does your sister think about it all?" Delilah changed the subject from her husband—and her breaking the promise that she wouldn't tell. I let it go, but only because I believed her when she said she hadn't said anything. I knew Jett could read her. I had watched it happen...

And it was a relief to know he wouldn't be spilling his thoughts to Luke.

"She thinks I should stay the fuck away from him," I answered her, standing to my feet. I glanced back at the disheveled covers, and suddenly the urge to run from the room came over me. "But I think I'm going to go for a walk on the beach. Wanna go?"

Delilah nodded. "I'm good with that. Jett went to breakfast with Luke, anyway."

"*Great*," I huffed, dread filling my chest. "Hopefully he still won't tell Luke."

"He won't," Delilah assured, leading the way to the door. "He hates drama way too much to get caught in the middle of that."

I laughed, knowing it was true. However, it didn't stop me from feeling the weight of my life choices. I had always fought the part of me that wanted Luke to know he was Autumn's father. The heartbroken, desperate part of me wanted to make him change his mind about me and come back. I spent so many nights wishing that the three of us could've been a family, but...

I never wanted him to make Autumn feel like she wasn't good enough.

The thought left a lump in my throat as I rode the elevator to the bottom floor with Delilah, the two of us falling into a comfortable silence. My eyes drifted toward the restaurant as we passed it, wondering if Luke and Jett were in there at that very moment, discussing what had happened between us last night.

"And, looks like we have trouble." Delilah's mutter caused my head to whip around just in time to see Xavier headed right for us, a snide look on his face.

*Oh shit...he looks pissed.*

"Good morning, ladies," he greeted us, though his eyes bore into mine like I was straight out of a bad dream.

"Hey." Delilah gave him a cheerful smile. "You missed a great night out on the yacht last night."

"Hmm, well, I would say you missed a great night with Layla and myself at the club, but that would be a *lie*, because *someone* flaked out."

*Oh no way.*

"Strippers just aren't really my thing," I said, folding my arms across my chest. The fact that we were even having this conversation made me feel like I was twenty-one again, arguing with a date as to *why* I had no interest in going to strip clubs.

"Wow, so you just bail with some possessive ex-boyfriend? I thought you were cool, Layla," he huffed, rolling his eyes. "It would've been a nice date."

"Uh..." My voice trailed off. "I never thought it was a date..."

"What else would it have been?"

"Two people hanging out," Delilah cut in. "This is just a trip for a bunch of friends."

"Yeah, well, interesting friend thing you have going on there with Luke," Xavier shot at me, his eyes glancing past me. "Must be hard to see your ex that you're clearly not over all over the place."

I opened my mouth to fire back at Xavier, but never had the chance, a blur whizzing past me followed by a pained groan from Xavier.

"What the hell, man?!" Xavier threw up his hands as I processed what was happening. Blood spurted from his nose as he shoved the chest of a red-faced Luke.

"Fuck you doing talking to her like that?" Luke barked back, shoving Xavier's chest again.

My mouth dropped open, flashbacks of the past playing in my head. "Luke, stop," I managed to choke out as Jett came rushing past me.

"Bro, don't," he demanded, but it didn't stop the fight.

"You just wanna fight, huh?" Xavier snapped back, his eyes on fire as he went straight for Luke, fist reared back.

*Oh my god.*

Luke stopped the punch, and I clenched my thighs—I had forgotten just how good of a fighter he was, and I hated that it turned me on. He went back at Xavier, but this time Xavier was ready. Delilah grabbed my arm and dragged me backward as the two went at each other...right in the middle of the lobby.

"We're so going to get kicked out." She let out a heavy sigh, shaking her head. "Stop them!" she called to Jett, who had retreated from the mess, shock all over his face.

My head fell to my hands as security came from nowhere, breaking the two of them apart, Jett jumping in then. Xavier was shouting expletives at Luke, his bloodied nose now paired with a fat lip. Luke spit blood back at him as a security guard and Jett jerked him back.

"Come on, dude, he's just a smartass," Jett growled, his words seeming to snap Luke out of it.

"You need to get your friend under control," Xavier shouted, shoving one of the security guards back. "This is insane, punching me over some piece of ass."

"Shut the fuck up!" Luke roared, lunging back at him.

"Calm down, sir," the security guard grunted, lugging him backward. "You two need to get your shit together before we call the cops."

"I could press charges for this," Xavier seethed, scowling at Luke before looking over at me. "And you should up your standards, for real."

I made a face but stayed silent. Luke was a bad idea, but Xavier was worse. Delilah squeezed my arm, reinforcing the idea to just let it go. Jett was busy trying to smooth it over with the guards, who appeared to be fuming about the mess.

"Let's just go on that walk while they settle this," Delilah said in a low voice as she tugged me toward the door. I nodded, stealing a glance over at Luke, who was staring at me. I opened my mouth, like I might say something to him, but turned away instead. I had no idea *what* to say to him...

"Hotheads." Delilah let out a sigh as we stepped outside, the sun instantly warming my skin. "I don't know why men always turn everything into a fight."

"I don't know," I agreed with her, glancing back to the lobby. As much as I wanted to say that what Luke had done was stupid...

It had my heart flip-flopping in my chest like a teenage girl.

# 14

# Luke

"Stupid move," Jett grumbled as we headed out of the security office. "I get that he was mouthing off, but the answer is never to go wailing on him. We're too old for this shit."

"Never too old to shut up a smartass."

"Nah, you and I both know you wouldn't have done shit had it not been Layla he was talking about." Jett's glare was menacing, but it didn't faze me.

Sure, it might have been a little immature, but I hated a man who would stoop low enough to insult a woman. The guy had no room to talk—he'd left Layla sitting there alone so he could have a lap dance from a stripper. And if his angle had been to make her jealous, I could guarantee it was a bad move. Strippers didn't make women jealous, they just pissed them the fuck off.

"At least we all get to stay," I offered up after a few quiet moments. "We could've all been forced to leave."

"Xavier *did* leave," Jett said through gritted teeth. "I get that you don't like him, but we used a lot of his clubs for our VIP events."

"I guess you might have to find an alternative. I'm sure Jackson has a few recommendations for that." I shrugged. My brother was a partier and rock star...he knew the best places.

Jett eyed me. "Yeah, well, you owe me for this one."

"Okay, so the next time you need a club for a VIP event, just let me know and I'll take care of it. No problem." My eyes drifted out toward the beach as we passed the door, and I wondered what Layla was up to—and just how pissed she was at me for that whole scuffle. It used to make her mad when we were younger, but it typically led to some amazing sex afterward. I doubted that would be the case this time...

But the thought was nice.

*Except I should let her go.*

"Fuck," I mumbled to myself under my breath as I stepped onto the elevator, both at the thought of Layla and at the way my knuckles were swelling.

"She fucking wrecks you, man," Jett chuckled, punching the second-floor button. "And you need to take some time to cool off. I get that you got your dick wet or whatever, and just like any other ex, I know that can fuck with your head...but Layla isn't just some girl you slept with a few times."

His words ground my nerves. "Why are you on *her* side?" I demanded, shaking my head. "Like, I get that what I did was shit, but I was *eighteen*. I didn't know my head from my ass at the time, and I've grown up a lot since then. I would think you of all people would know that."

"That's the thing," Jett said with a sigh as the doors slid open. "I *do* know that. I know you're a great guy now—and you've worked out most of that shit with your family. However, ever since you showed up here, you've got your head back up your ass. You just got in a *fight* for fuck's sake."

I cringed, thinking over my choices since I had laid my eyes on Layla. "Maybe I should get my head together," I admitted, feeling more and more like an idiot. "She just makes me feel like a fuckin' kid again."

"Yeah, well, that's something you need to address and think through, but regardless, you *don't* need to be getting into anymore trouble. One call to the family lawyer is enough to set off the red flags in your family."

I nodded, stopping just outside my room. "Yeah, I get what you're saying. I'll lay off."

"Dude." Jett clamped a hand on each of my shoulders, leveling with me. "Just take a freaking breath. Maybe you need to come to terms with the idea that you don't dislike the woman—maybe you're still in love with her."

I shook my head, but the memory of the feelings that had crept in during sex came to my mind. "I don't know. It's fine. I just need to take a few hours to get my shit together."

"Good idea." Jett released me, and I stepped inside, shutting the door. I let out a frustrated groan as soon as the door closed behind me. I *was* acting like an idiot—a jealous, possessive idiot. And for what reason? To make Layla miserable while she was here?

I ran my fingers through my hair and plopped down on the bed. I hadn't been back to my room since last night with Layla, and I knew I was overdue for a shower. However, before I gave in to that urge, I pulled out my phone. I was pretty sure I had been blocked from all of Layla's social media accounts, but I was still curious about her company—except I had no idea what it was called.

So I googled her name followed by cosmetics.

*Woman Builds Cosmetic Empire Overnight*

"Damn," I commented after reading the title of the first article to pop up. I clicked on it, and immediately a bright and smiling Layla loaded on my screen. I pored over the article, seeing that she had founded the brand based on her skin being sensitive and how it had gone further than she'd expected to.

She was a fucking millionaire now.

Pride swelled in my chest as I finished reading it. Layla had made a name for herself by following her passion, and I couldn't be happier for her. I knew that she would be something special—and it didn't take becoming a millionaire to be that—but the way she had hustled was beyond impressive.

I scrolled through her website, checking out all of her products. I had no interest or idea about what made great makeup, but she seemed to have it figured out based on the good reviews and sales of her products. I closed out of it after a few moments and tossed my phone onto the bed beside me.

*I have to get my shit together.*

For the last six years, I had been suppressing the heartbreak I'd endured—but honestly it had started when we broke up a decade ago. I had never wanted to end things...

And now I wished I hadn't.

My phone vibrated on the bed beside me, and I halfway expected it to be my father. Our family lawyer, Greg, had gotten a call from me today—and he usually ratted us out to our dad. Client confidentiality didn't exist when it came to the family. However, as I picked it up, I was somewhat relieved to see my brother's name.

"What's up, Jackson?" I asked, relaxing back on the pillows.

"Have you looked over the label's financials?"

I let out a sigh. "I have, and they appear to be in good shape, but I don't know if I want to do it. You know as well as I do that Eli doesn't have time to pick up another company. Whiss Productions has a full enough schedule as it is. If he stays invested in it physically, he can't take on anything else."

"Okay, but what about you?" Jackson countered. "You're not involved in really any of the businesses that you have stake in."

"Wrong," I snapped, shaking my head. "I'm involved in all of them, which is why I seriously have no fucking time to pick up a record label. I know that all you see is creative freedom with your music—and I get that—but I don't know that I'm the right partner for you."

"I could run it myself," he argued, his voice straining. "You think I'm just some piece of shit who parties all the time, but that's not who I am anymore. I can't keep up with that lifestyle, and the road doesn't exactly make for the best family life."

"Wait, what?" I couldn't hide the surprise from my tone. "Since when are you thinking of starting a family? All I've heard from you is that your band is the only family you need."

"Well, things change. When you know you know—or something like that."

I sat up, my brows furrowed with curiosity. "So, you've met someone?"

"Yeah, I think so."

"Damn." I paused, taking it in for a second. "I never thought I'd hear you say that. Congrats, man. Is she a good woman?"

"Yeah, I think so. Well, we're figuring it out, but yeah. Ever since Eli settled down, and they had their kid, that's all I want. I know our family life was dysfunctional, but man, I want a family."

Something tugged at my emotions, and I fought it off. "You should have whatever you want. It'd be good for you to settle down, anyway."

"Yeah, what about you? I was with Dad this afternoon and he got a call from Greg. I hate to say it, man, but that's the first time you've done a piece of stupid shit in a long time. You're lucky that dude you decked didn't press charges."

*Great, so Greg* did *blab the news to the whole family.*

"Uh, yeah, I've been an idiot."

"Yeah, why?"

"Why the hell are you so nosy?" I snapped, not in the mood to go there with him. He had no room to talk, anyway.

"Oh, come on, I swear Jett just brings out the fighting side of you. You were always getting into fights in high school. Mom thought she was doing something real fucking smart when she sent you off to that boarding school for geniuses or whatever, but all she did was set you up for problems."

I hesitated, trying to decide if I wanted to go there—but other than Jett, Jackson *was* my closest friend, brother or not. "It wasn't Jett that had me fighting all the time."

"Huh? What's that supposed to mean?"

"Do you remember…" My voice trailed off as I lost some confidence. Did it even matter about Layla if there was nothing there between the two of us?

"Do I remember what? I was like fucking twelve when you graduated. I don't remember shit."

"You have the worst mouth, bro," I scolded him. "But do you remember Layla Miller?"

"*Oh.*"

"What's that supposed to mean?" I demanded, my heart jumping at the way he responded.

"You mean the hot friend that you had tons of pictures with on social media? She was with Jett, right?"

"No…she was never with Jett."

"Okay, so what? She caused you to get into a bunch of fights in high school? Was she starting a bunch of drama or some shit?"

"She's here," I said, picking at the lint on my shorts.

"So, you got into a fight with a sleazy club owner because of her? Dude, I'm not following you. You're gonna have to start fucking talking because—"

"I dated her all through high school, Jackson. We started dating when I was sixteen, and we didn't break up until Mom threw that fit about me not going to Harvard when I enrolled at UCLA."

He was quiet on the other end for a few long moments. "I thought you never had a girlfriend in high school."

"I lied."

"Why?"

"You know the pressure Mom put on me when it came to girls..."

"Oh right," he snorted. "Must be of high society or you'd be disowned. Ironic how she disowned us anyway. You really care about Layla?"

"Yeah," I said in a low voice, realizing just how fucking emotional I felt talking about her to my family for the first time in my entire life. "Yeah, I thought she was the one, but I didn't want to put her through Mom."

"I don't blame you."

"We hooked up once when she came to New York about six years ago, but she ran out before we could talk. Maybe I'm not over it."

"Maybe you should tell her that."

"I should probably just save her the trouble and let her go." I hated what I was saying, but I had already made myself look like an asshole.

"I think you should just avoid getting into fights and show her that you're not a kid anymore. Go be the grown-ass Luke that owns a million fucking businesses."

I rolled my eyes. "I don't own a million businesses."

He laughed. "You get what I'm saying. Fix it."

# 15

## *Layla*

"So she starts kindergarten the second week of August?" Delilah asked me, setting her book in her lap. "I can't believe she's already starting school."

"I know." I pooched out my bottom lip. "I can't believe it either. It feels like she's just growing up so fast. I can't stand it. I want her to slow the hell down some days."

"Won't be long and you'll be sending her off to college," Jett mused, his own face buried in a book of his own. It was some sort of military thriller—not my style at all, but to each their own. I had been surprised when he'd shown up not long after the ordeal, and I'd been wondering about Luke...

But I didn't want to pry.

"Are we taking the yacht out tonight?" Delilah asked, letting out a yawn. "I could use a night under the stars."

"And I could use a night without the anxiety of whether or not that piece of shit will actually get us back to shore."

I laughed at the two of them, both giving each other glares. "You could just compromise, and we just stay in the harbor. We'd probably have no problem making it back."

"But you can't see the stars as well," Delilah pointed out, her nose scrunching up. "And that's my favorite part."

"It's impossible for her to compromise," Jett grumbled, picking his book back up from his chair. We were sitting three in a row, and the more I thought about it, the more I realized just how much of a third wheel I really was.

"Well, I say we just tempt fate and take the boat out." I shrugged my shoulders, shooting Delilah a wink.

"You can always push Luke from the deck. Much less likely to find the body out in open waters."

Jett nearly dropped his book. "You two need to slow down on the true crime docs before you get arrested and charged with conspiracy."

"Oh stop," Delilah chided him. "You know as well as I do that the guy deserves to be dumped overboard—you could throw him the life preserver."

He rolled his eyes as she giggled. "You know, he's not that bad of a guy. Granted, you"—he looked at me—"bring out the stupid in him, and you always have, but he's grown up a lot in the last decade."

*Not that I've seen.*

I kept my reply to myself, however. There was no point in arguing with Jett. He knew Luke better than I did—nowadays, anyway. "How has he grown up?" I might be able to keep my attitude in check, but my curiosity had gone unhinged.

"I'm not discussing this." He eyed me. "If you want to know, maybe you should have an actual conversation with him instead of just skipping to the sex part. You *both* have some life changes that could be addressed."

# LAYLA

My jaw dropped, knowing exactly what he was insinuating. "I didn't—"

He held up his hand and let out a sigh. "I have my suspicions, but I don't need them confirmed. It's your life, and you have to figure it out. I'm not getting involved. If you want my advice, on the other hand, I'm more than happy to give it to you."

I frowned. "I don't even want to know what you think."

"I think you *both* are about as fucked-up as you could be," Jett mumbled, shaking his head, though a smile tugged at his lips. "And my wife probably knows way more about it than I do."

"I'm pretty sure no one knows as much as you," Delilah said, her tone teasing. However, her smile faded as she looked past me. "But speaking of pompous assholes, it looks like Luke has finally decided to join us while everyone else does their own thing."

*Great.*

My heart kicked off in my chest, thrumming away as I adjusted my sunglasses and pretended to be immersed in a shitty romance book. I didn't want Luke to think that I was bothered in the slightest...even if his presence rattled every nerve in my body.

"Hey." His voice was deep and a little uneven.

"I take it you iced those hands of yours?" Jett chuckled, offering a beer. "Everyone else is doing god knows what, so nice of you to join us."

"Yeah, I don't know *everyone else*, so my choices are limited. You know I prefer the company of people I actually know."

"Right," I snorted, unable to hold back my comment.

"Actually though, could we talk?"

I felt his eyes on me, and I forced myself to look up from the blurry words. "Me?" I pointed to my chest, accentuated by a red bikini top.

His face flashed with irritability, but it only lasted a second. "Yeah, *you*."

I shrugged my shoulders, setting my book down and turning to Delilah. "Will you make sure you take that back to my room if I'm not back in time?"

She smiled, her eyes only slightly tinged with concern. "Of course."

"Thanks." I let out a sigh and grabbed my cover-up, shrugging the white fabric over my sightly tanned—but mostly burned—skin. "Let's go," I said to Luke, gesturing for him to lead the way.

"Make good choices, kids," Jett called after us, and I rolled my eyes.

Luke chuckled, shaking his head. "He's always been like that, you know."

"And you've always been one to start fights," I retorted, inwardly cringing at the sparring I still tended to dish out. I needed to calm down and make friends...

But nothing more than that.

*Don't forget about Autumn.*

That still hadn't changed. I needed to stay strong, no matter how much my pussy ached at the sight of those hazel eyes.

"I'm not the kind to get into fights," Luke began, letting out a heavy breath. "I think you should know that."

"You've *always* been the kind to get into fights," I immediately countered. "The last time I saw you in NYC, you got into a fight."

"A dude copped a feel of you!" he snapped, shaking his head. "It was completely warranted—and I didn't fight him. I just gave him one good punch. He got thrown out, not me."

"Still, violence isn't the answer," I said with a shrug, hating to recall anything about that night. We both knew what happened after that moment, and it wasn't something I wanted to relive.

Luke's jaw tensed. "I know it isn't. I had a lot of anger issues back in school, and that's why I fought the way I did. But also...I was so worried about losing you."

"Yeah, because you refused to put a label on our relationship. It was like the whole fucking school knew that we were together—but we *weren't* together."

"We *were* together," he argued with me, his voice taking a plunge. "And you know we were. I told you about the issues I had with my family."

"Ah, right," I snorted, growing defensive. "Still blaming them for your inability to commit?"

"Jesus, Layla," he said, exasperated, throwing his hands in the air. "I wanted to apologize for the way I've been acting, and you're still stuck in the past. I'm not the same kid I was ten years ago. I've changed."

"You still punched—"

"I *know*," he cut me off. "I just fell into old habits. I wanted to protect you from the scumbag that I knew Xavier to be. You deserve better than that guy—I mean, he left you for a lap dance with a stripper. That's low."

I chewed on my bottom lip, unable to argue with that. "Okay, you make a good point—but the fight wasn't cool."

"No, it wasn't." Luke's shoulders relaxed as he glanced down to his bruised knuckles. "But I hated the way he spoke to you. He wasn't looking out for you, he was just being an asshole."

I nodded, wrapping my arms around myself. "Yeah, I know...but I can handle myself. I've aways been able to handle myself."

"I know." His voice dropped to a near whisper as he grabbed my hand, both of us stopping at the edge of the pier. I glanced around, realizing that we had walked far from the thick crowds on the white sands. "Layla, I know you've always been able to handle yourself—and you've made a name for yourself. I always knew you would. Your business is really something."

I felt a blush creeping into my cheeks. "Did you look it up?"

"Yeah. Granted, I didn't get very far. You've got me blocked on every site known to man. I could only see the website."

*Autumn.*

"I know, sorry," I said, not offering up more of an explanation. "I've been living the last ten years trying to pretend like you don't exist."

"Well, unfortunately, I *do*. And we share a common friend. We can't keep causing so much trouble for him."

I narrowed my eyes. "You mean, *you* can't keep causing trouble for him."

Luke chuckled, his eyes lighting up the way they used to—back when we were in love. "Yeah, I guess maybe I have been the troublemaker. I was lucky I didn't get cuffed and stuffed today."

"Friends in high places," I teased, poking him in the chest. My eyes drifted down his toned pectoral muscles showing through his white T-shirt. The man had the body of a Greek god—I would never tell him that, though.

"Greg always gets us out of sticky situations." His fingers wrapped around my hand, still pressing into his chest.

*Oops.*

Electricity shot through his warm touch, the breeze blowing off the water not enough to cool the fire sparking between us. Everything in my brain was screaming at me to pull away, to not give in to the few moments of pleasant conversation that we had. I didn't want to fall back into old habits—I'd already fucked up twice since showing up here...

*But I've already fucked up—what's one more time?*

Ugh, my mind was not reliable.

"I'm sorry, Layla." Luke's eyes met mine, and the genuine remorse in them rocked my heart—if only he would say that about what had happened ten years ago. "I shouldn't have started the fight, and I shouldn't have been such a jealous asshole."

I swallowed hard, my brain spinning out of control as he closed what little distance was between us. What was I supposed to be doing? Everything faded to mush as my eyes landed on his lips.

"It's okay," I breathed out, though I wasn't sure *why* it was okay. Nothing was okay. I was hiding a kid from him for heaven's sake.

*Run away, Layla.*

The little angel on my shoulder was screaming at me as Luke's hand wrapped around my waist.

"Maybe we should start this trip over." Luke's voice was soft, sounding like music in my ears. "And see where this goes."

*No, no, no.*

But my body was doing everything that my mind wasn't. Moisture was pooling between my legs, and my hands were drifting up his shoulders, his neck, and didn't stop until they were tugging his face down to mine.

This man made me lose my fucking mind.

And no matter what I tried to tell myself, I liked it.

# 16

## Luke

"*Ooh...*" Layla let out a moan as I buried my face in the nape of her neck, my hands pushing the white cover-up off her shoulders. The moment the door of my room had closed, I was all over her. As tempting as it had been to take her right there by the pier...

I wasn't willing to risk someone seeing.

"Get this off," Layla panted, trying to pull my T-shirt up and over my head. I helped her efforts, pulling my lips from her skin long enough to slip off the cotton material and launch it across the room.

"I like this on you." I pointed to the bikini she had on, the red material barely covering her tits. "But I think it'd look better on the floor."

Layla giggled, reaching behind her back and undoing the string. I watched her with eagle eyes as I took off my swim trunks, letting my throbbing cock free. Layla's breasts bounced as she dropped the top on her white cover-up.

"Take those off too," I instructed, fighting the urge to stroke myself as I watched her strip down to nothing for me.

She bit her lip as she met my eyes, shimmying out of the bottoms. Her bare body was sun-kissed, but also a little red. I'd have to keep that in mind when I was fucking her. I took a step toward her, but before I could reach out and snag her back into my arms, she dropped to her knees, getting eye level with my cock.

*Oh fuck...*

The woman was a fucking goddess when it came to blow jobs—she always had been—even when we were both just trying to figure sex out back in high school. Layla tipped her head up at me, running her tongue along her bottom lip, and then drifted forward.

The head of my dick was swelling with the need for her hot, wet mouth to take it in, but she teased me, gently brushing the pad of her tongue against it. She removed the precum and then met my gaze.

"What do you want me to do, Luke?" Her voice was sultry and heavy with lust, coming out in a purr as her fingers ran down my thighs.

"Suck my fucking cock," I answered her with a strong tone, but my body shivered at her touch. "I want it down your throat."

"*Ooh.*" She licked her lips again, and one of her hands migrated to the base of my dick, wrapping around it. "I like the sound of that."

Anticipation was building in my abdomen, the muscles tightening as she ran a circle around my tip. "I'd like the sound of your mouth on it," I said, followed by a groan as her hot breath encircled it.

"It's so big," she whimpered, before finally taking in the first half of it. My breath hitched as the pleasure mounted, and my hands went for her hair, pulling it away from her face as she worked her way down. She kept one hand on my thigh and the other on the base of my cock. I knew I was gifted when it came to size, and I never pushed any woman to take the whole thing...

But Layla *always* did.

"Fuck, baby, just like that," I growled as I slid down the back of her throat, a gagging noise following. She came off of it, looking up at me with watery eyes, before doing it again. I let her have control, my hands only serving to ensure my view.

"Your cock is so good," she purred as she caught her breath before going back to sucking me off. She picked up her pace, using her hand too so that she could cover the whole thing faster and without losing her ability to breathe.

Groans and sharp breaths came from me as the pleasure intensified, my muscles beginning to stiffen. "I'm gonna cum in that pretty little mouth."

Layla moaned in reply, continuing at the same vigorous pace. Her plan was to take me over the edge—and I couldn't be more fucking okay with that. My hands tightened in her hair as my hips gave in to the need to thrust, working with her motions to do the final stretch. A deep, guttural growl rolled off my tongue as I exploded, emptying myself into her mouth.

She leaned back, opening to show me my cum, and then swallowed it, leaving me shivering with primal arousal. "You taste so good."

My cock was still hard as I pulled her to her feet. "You taste even better, and I'm fucking dying to put that pussy in my mouth," I said in a husky voice. I lifted her off the ground and took her straight to the bed, letting her go.

She smiled seductively at me as I climbed over her, locking our lips together for a hot kiss. She still had the salty taste of me on her lips as my tongue invaded her mouth, and it was like claiming my fucking territory.

I wanted her to *always* have me on her lips—and in her pussy.

My mouth broke from hers and I made my way down her body, not even remotely bothered by the remnants of the ocean I tasted, the grit of sand being the most prolific one. She moaned out with pleasure as I sucked her tit into my mouth, running my tongue around her areola and then her nipple.

"So fucking pretty," I murmured as I covered every inch of her body. My hands roamed, but I kept trailing downward, kissing across her stomach. She caught her breath as I finally reached her pelvis. Lifting my head, I moved to her inner thighs, kissing each one before I ran my tongue in between her folds.

"Oh my god!" she cried out.

"You're so wet for me," I growled in satisfaction, lapping up the moisture that had pooled. I drank her juices, reveling in the way she tasted and smelled. It was almost like coming home when I ate her out. I had spent a lot of time between her legs when we were together, and it was the best fucking thing I had ever experienced.

"Just keep doing that," Layla panted as her hips worked against my face, my tongue gyrating against her clit. "You're so good at this."

"Tell me how good I am, Layla," I growled, pressing my tongue to her entrance.

"You're so fucking good, Luke," she whimpered, squirming against me as I continued. "Oh my god, you're so fucking good."

My mouth trailed back up to her clit, sucking the little bean gently into my mouth as my fingers replaced my tongue. I wanted to fill every inch of her body with me, and as I fingered her with two, I let a third tease her ass. I knew she didn't want any more than that, and I wouldn't push her—but I was going to fucking make her think about it.

And know that I was *everywhere* on her body.

Moans filled the room as she ground against me, more moisture slipping from her pussy as I worked to bring her to ecstasy. My cock was throbbing and feeling the need to fill her tight little pussy, but I focused on Layla. I'd get my fill of her as soon as she came all over my face.

"*Oh, oh!*" she cried out as she clenched around me, her thighs clenching and trapping my head where it was. "I'm gonna...I'm gonna..."

"Cum for me," I growled, finishing the phrase for her. "Cum all over my fuckin' face, Layla."

She cried out in response, her body beginning to pulse around me. "Luke!" Moisture filled my mouth, gushing as she rode the high of her orgasm. I lapped it up, nearly exploding at the sheer amount she had given me.

*Fuck, this woman is perfect.*

Her fingers loosened as she came down and I finished cleaning her up with my tongue, leaving nothing uncovered. Her breaths were still shaky as I lifted myself from between her legs, reaching across her body to the nightstand. I had bought a box of condoms and shoved it there, just in case—and now I was really glad I had. I pulled one out and tore it open.

"Let me do it," she said, her eyes flashing with lust as she took the wrapper from my hand. I leaned over and kissed her, giving her a little taste of herself as she pulled the latex from the package. She licked her lips as I pulled away, and I let out a groan as she stretched the condom over my length, giving me a squeeze.

"God, I just wanna bury this inside of you," I growled as she released me, and situated myself in between her legs.

"Then do it," she said, her expression daring.

"I'm gonna fuck you so hard that all you remember is me," I continued as I ran the tip of my dick into her slit.

She whimpered, her body trembling. "You're all I ever remember."

The words hit me, causing me to pause for a moment, my tip lingering right at the entrance of her pussy. I met her gaze, seeing the sincerity in her eyes.

*Fuck, she means it.*

Emotions threatened to swell, making the fuck turn into something more than I intended it to be. I suppressed them by sliding into her, the tight, wet pussy enough to take my mind off the heaviness of her words. She moaned, shifting her hips.

"Give me more," she pleaded as I stopped at only halfway, pulling it back out. "Please. Fuck me."

"I like it when you beg for my cock." I smirked, my dick pulsing with arousal as I met her disappointed expression. "Tell me how bad you want it."

Her eyes caught fire. "I want you so fucking bad, baby," she cooed. "So. Fucking. Bad."

I let out a groan and plunged my entire length into her, my hips coming flush to hers. "You're so tight."

She moaned as I rocked against her, thrusting in and out of her pussy. I reached for her legs and placed them on my shoulders, pausing only to kiss her calves as I did so. My hands made an iron grip on her tiny waist, and I hungrily watched her tits bounce as I mercilessly ravaged her body.

"*Fuck*!" Layla's face contorted with pleasure as I pounded her, my breaths growing long and deep as my heart hammered in my chest. The sounds of our bodies slapping and our satisfied, lustful noises penetrated the air around us as the smell of our sex grew stronger.

Layla's eyes squeezed shut. "I'm gonna cum," she moaned, wriggling against my grasp. I reached in between her legs and began to stimulate her clit as my cock slid in and out of her. Within just moments, she was crying out my name and pulsing around my dick.

And it was enough to send me right over the edge with her.

I growled, dropping her legs and collapsing forward as I released, stilling my body as my cock did the final amount of work. Layla moaned at the sensation, still coming down from her own high. Her eyes fluttered open, meeting mine, and I leaned down to kiss her lips. She kissed me back, clinging to me like she used to…

And all the emotions I had suppressed during sex came rushing back.

There was no way to get around it—I wasn't fucking Layla because I just needed to get laid. I was fucking her because I still wanted her just as bad as I had all those years ago. I pulled out of her, and as I cleaned up, she slid off the bed and headed for the bathroom.

*And now, she's gonna leave.*

I pushed away the thought, reminding myself that even though I'd alluded to starting over—like maybe a relationship—she had made it clear with her actions that she didn't want that from me. I was probably just going to be a fling…

And I had to be okay with that.

"Hey." She popped her head out of the bathroom. "Are you hungry?"

The question surprised me. "Yeah, I could eat."

"Cool, let's order room service."

# 17

## Layla

I lay in the bed next to Luke, listening to his deep, steady breathing. I had been tempted to ask questions about the past, but I'd held back while we ate and watched a movie. I figured I wouldn't ruin the two of us getting along...

For now, anyway.

I stared at the ceiling above us, cuddled up in one of his T-shirts and nothing else. Not once had it crossed my mind to slip back to my room and get a change of clothes, but it was fine. I'd just have to do it in the morning.

*You're being dumb.* I could hear Lily's voice in my head as I shut my eyes. I could only imagine what else she'd say if she knew about me falling into him again. There was just something that always felt so right about us—and maybe it was the fact that he was my first, making the connection more intense or something...

*Or maybe it's all the feelings.*

"Nope," I muttered to myself, shaking my head as I blatantly lied. I knew the truth. My phone lighting up on the nightstand grabbed my attention, and I reached for it, seeing none other than my sister's name on the screen. Before I answered, I slid out of bed and headed for the balcony.

"Hey," she greeted me as I shut the door behind me, taking in the warm breeze and view of the ocean. "Your daughter won't go to bed until she tells you goodnight, apparently."

I smiled, my heart squeezing as I thought of my sweet Autumn. "That's okay, I always have time to tell her goodnight."

"You sound happy," Lily said, drawing out the words in suspicion. "Is there anything you need to tell me?"

Biting the inside of my cheek so hard I tasted copper, I let out a sigh. "I don't know."

"Oh god, you slept with him again," she groaned. "I swear, Layla, have you seriously forgotten just how badly he broke your heart? And what about Autumn?"

"What about me?" I heard my daughter in the background.

"Just a second," Lily said to her, before lowering her voice. "You just watch out for yourself and make sure that if this is seriously something you want to pursue, he's ready to toe the line. Got it?"

I nearly rolled my eyes at the way she mothered me. "I got it."

"Okay." She let out a relieved sigh. "Here's your mommy, Autumn."

"Hi, Mommy," Autumn's sweet voice came over the line, loud and clear. "I don't want to go to bed."

"Well, you need to go to bed," I countered. "You'll be *really* tired in the morning if you don't, and I know you have lots of plans with Aunt Lily."

# LAYLA

"Yeah, I guess so," she grumbled, nearly causing me to laugh. "I just miss you. Aunt Lily's bedtime stories aren't nearly as good."

"Well, I'll be home before you know it. You get some sleep and maybe tomorrow I can tell you a story. It's too late tonight."

"Okay," she said with a sigh. "I love you."

"I love you too. Goodnight."

"Night," she chirped, and then the phone shuffled and I heard little footsteps disappear.

"Well, that was just too easy," Lily laughed. "I thought I was never going to get her in bed tonight. Good to know I just have to call you." She paused when I didn't immediately say anything. "I just want you to watch out for your heart, Layla. It's not that I don't want you to be happy or enjoy yourself. I just...I'm so leery of Luke and all the history you have with him—and Autumn."

"I know, I know," I said, my voice growing quiet. "There's just still...there's still something there."

"Just be careful exploring that," Lily replied. "And make him work for it."

*He has been.*

"Okay," I said instead. "I'll call you tomorrow."

"Deal. Love you."

"You too," I said, eyeing the balcony door as I hung up. Hopefully, Luke hadn't heard any of that conversation. The last thing I needed was another confrontation about a stupid phone call. I made my way back inside of his room, relieved to hear his still steady breaths. Creeping across the floor, I sat my phone back down and crawled into the bed.

Part of me wanted to escape to my own room for the safety of my heart, but there was another part of me that didn't want to bail on him in the same way I had before. I mean, I could still insist that it was just a fling in the morning light...right?

I shut my eyes, not feeling an ounce of fatigue as my mind started to race. I took a few deep breaths, memories threatening to replay. I squeezed my eyes tighter, but no matter how hard I tried, they wouldn't relent...

*"Okay, so Brittany Riggs is throwing a massive end-of-summer party at her place," Jett said, staring down at his cell phone before looking up at us. "I think we should go."*

*I crinkled my nose. "Do we have to? I mean, her parties are fine, but I swear there's always so many younger kids there—we're leaving for college in like two weeks."*

*Luke's arm stiffened around my shoulders. "Is that all there is?"*

*"Yeah." I looked up at him, furrowing my brows. "And I'm counting down the days until we're far, far away from this place. Then, we can be out about us."*

*He nodded but didn't say anything to me, turning to Jett. "Maybe we should just skip the party tonight."*

*Jett cocked his head sideways. "Why? There's literally nothing else to do tonight, and Sarah's gonna be there."*

*"Oh my god," I groaned at the mention of her name. "You really need to just let that go. We're leaving for Cali in literally two weeks, and Sarah is not worth it."*

*"Yeah, but she's worth one last lay," Jett chuckled, shooting me a smirk. "I think that's a good enough reason for me. If you wanna get laid, you just have to hit up Luke. I've literally been in the desert all fucking summer."*

*"You're such a pig." I scrunched up my nose at him as I leaned into Jett. "You know women don't actually* like *guys who have been with a million women, right? Like, wait for love."*

*"You're just saying that because you've only ever been with Luke—and he's only ever been with you," Jett quipped, shaking his head at the two of us. "You two don't know there's way more to explore."*

*"Dude, just shut up." Luke laughed, squeezing me. "You're sounding like a pervert. Not everyone wants to get STDs like you."*

*"Whatever." Jett slid off my bed, rolling his eyes. "I'm going to this damn party. Are you guys coming or not?"*

*I bit my lip, knowing I would have to slide past Lily, who was supposed to be keeping an eye on me while my parents were on a last-minute business trip. "I guess we could go." I shrugged, looking up at Luke, who was making a face. "It is the last party of the summer."*

*"Yeah, but I was really hoping to spend the night with you...since your parents aren't here."*

*"Good luck with that," I snorted. "Lily will run you out with a kitchen knife."*

*"Solid fucking point." Luke grimaced. "Let's just go to the party."*

*"That's what I'm talking about," Jett said, grinning at us. "Our last night here in this hellhole, then it's off to bigger and better things."*

*"Like actually calling you my boyfriend," I teased, poking Luke in the ribs as he unwound from me. "It'll be a such good feeling."*

*"Yeah, for sure," he said, his eyes avoiding mine as he stretched his arms over his head. My stomach swirled at his demeanor, but I brushed it off. There was nothing that could ruin the high of our impending future.*

*"Just give me a few minutes to get ready," I said, heading for the bathroom.*

\*\*\*

*The music blared over the speakers, and I sipped on something fruity from a red solo cup. "I don't know where Jett went off to," I said to Luke, having to nearly yell as bodies bumped against us.*

*"Let's go outside," Luke shouted back to me, grabbing my hand and leading me out the back sliding door. As he shut the door, the music became nothing but bass rattling the glass. "I don't know how she manages to have these parties and the cops never get called."*

*"I don't know." I shrugged, letting him lead me around the landscaped path that led to a gazebo with a swing. Every time we came to Brittany's house, we always ended up in the same spot, and my thighs clenched as my mind replayed the things we had done out here.*

*"I hope Jett isn't fucking Sarah."*

*Luke's comment was unsurprising. He hated Sarah—with good reason. She treated Jett like trash, always using him for whatever she wanted, but never committing to him. She was the stereotypical reason that young relationships didn't work.*

*"I keep thinking he's going to learn his lesson," I added, taking a seat on the wooden swing. "But I swear he never does."*

*"I guess that's what happens when it's a good lay," Luke said blankly, shrugging his shoulders.*

*"Oh? So is that why you're with me?" I questioned him, my voice playful. I knew he loved me. Our sex was just a bonus.*

*"No, and you know that," he countered in a flat tone.*

*I furrowed my brow at him, having noticed his strange mood the entire night. "What's going on with you? Did you get in another fight with your parents?"*

*He was quiet, his eyes dropping to his hands in his lap. "I wouldn't say it like that..."*

*My heart sank in my chest. "Then what is it? What happened? I thought everything was fine. We're leaving for college in two weeks..." He nodded, but the way he wasn't looking at me was starting to worry me. "Luke, just tell me what happened. Don't shut down. I hate it when you shut down."*

*He looked up at me then, his eyes glistening under the moonlight. "I think we need to talk about everything, Layla..."*

*"What's that supposed to mean?" I instantly went on the defense, my stomach starting to feel sick with dread. "What did they say about me this time?"*

*"They didn't say anything about you..."*

*"Then what is it?" I demanded, feeling my voice strain. "Just tell me what the fuck it is you need to say."*

*"I can't do this." His voice was barely audible.*

*"What can't you do?" I choked out. Surely, he couldn't mean...*

*"I'm not going to UCLA, Layla."*

*"What?!" I felt like I was bursting at the seams. "Where are you going? So you were lying about it this whole time?"*

*He shook his head. "No, I wasn't. I was planning to go to UCLA, but then my parents told me they'd cut me off if I didn't go to Harvard."*

*My heart began to hammer in my chest. "But...but that's on the other side of the country, Luke. I thought...I thought we had it figured out. We were going to live in the dorms for our freshman year and then move in together..."*

*His head fell into his hands. "I can't do that. We can't do that."*

*"We can make long distance work, then." My voice trembled as I reached for him, but he pulled away.*

*"No, we can't."*

*"Are you breaking up with me?" Tears crested my eyes, slipping down my cheeks. "I thought...I thought you loved me."*

*He was quiet, and his silence was the answer.*

*It was over.*

# 18

## Luke

"I think I'm gonna hit the gym this morning," Layla said to me as she emerged from the bathroom, her dark hair pulled up in a messy bun. She still had on just my T-shirt, and the sight was one I had missed.

"Yeah? I didn't know you were into the gym." I chuckled, though by the looks of her toned legs, it made a lot of sense. "I think I'm gonna skip it this morning."

She smiled, but it didn't reach her eyes. "I don't blame you." Layla went for the pile of her clothes—well, bathing suit—and headed back into the bathroom. Something was off with her, and as much as I wanted to ask, I was clinging to the fact she wasn't running out.

I flipped the covers back, my mind replaying the shower we had taken together the night before. Nothing had happened during it, but it felt nearly as intimate as the sex that had led up to it. I smiled as I pulled on a pair of khaki shorts and a pale-blue button up. There was no doubt that I was on a high...

And I wasn't giving up on Layla—even if there was still some lingering fear.

Rolling my shoulders, I let the hope settle in my chest as she reemerged, wearing the bathing suit and cover-up from the day before. My cock came to life in my pants, and part of me considered taking her right back to bed...

But I didn't.

"I'm gonna just head to my room and change, and then I'll see you later," she said, her voice light but her face devoid of emotion. "I think Delilah and Jett are eating breakfast downstairs again. She told me to let you know. I'm going to just grab a smoothie after my workout."

I nodded, still sensing that something was off. "That sounds good. Maybe we can hang out this afternoon? I got a phone call scheduled with my brother for later this morning," I said with a sigh, inwardly dreading the meeting with Eli, Jackson, and my dad over the stupid record label Jackson was determined to buy.

"Yeah, we can do that." She gave me one more look before heading out of the room, the door shutting softly behind her. I finished getting ready before I headed out too, glancing back at the bed one last time.

The hallway was empty as I made my way to the restaurant, which was very much the opposite. It took me a second to spot Jett and Delilah, but I was relieved to see that they were there alone, none of Jett's friends or business associates with him.

"Hey," I greeted them, taking a seat. They must've just gotten there, since neither of them had anything other than a water in front of them.

"Hey, hey." Jett gave me a sly look, and I rolled my eyes. "What's your plans for today?"

"I don't know." I shrugged. "I do have a call with my family later this morning, but that's it. I guess being on vacation means there's *no* plans. Isn't that the point of it?"

"For some," Delilah muttered, taking a sip of her water. "If you're like Jett, you can never just relax and enjoy the break. He's always gotta be doing something. We're going into the city to go shopping today, though."

"Yeah, that sounds like something I'm gonna pass on," I said, though as soon as the words left my mouth, I wondered if Layla would be joining them. She wasn't much of a shopper when I knew her best, but things changed. Well, some things did, anyway.

"Layla said the same thing," Jett said with a smirk. "I wonder why..."

My heart flip-flopped in my chest. "We didn't make any plans for the day, really. Nothing other than hanging out this afternoon..."

"That sounds like making plans to me," Delilah snorted. "You don't have to downplay it. If you have real feelings for her then admit it." Her bluntness was surprising, and it must've surprised Jett too, based on the nudge she got under the table.

I used the moment as an out. "I thought about taking her out on the yacht," I said, which was mostly thinking aloud. I hadn't really thought it through.

"Yeah, that would be fine." Jett waved at the waitress, signaling for her to come over. "Just watch the engine. I know you have a lot of experience with them, but I don't want to see the two of you having to call for help."

Delilah laughed. "Can you imagine? Being stranded on the boat?"

"I'd rather not," I grunted.

# LUKE

"So, where did you and Layla run off to yesterday?" Jett jumped the subject back to her. "It felt like old times. The two of you were always running off and doing god knows what."

*Fucking like rabbits.*

"We just hung out," I answered, even though based on the looks on their faces, they knew *exactly* what we had done. "The room service is pretty good here," I added, just as the waitress showed back up.

"What can I get for you?" she asked me.

"Just a water and the omelet," I answered her, before letting Delilah and Jett also order their breakfast. My mind wandered back to Layla—would she want to go out on the yacht? The ocean had never really been her thing, but I also knew that she'd always said she loved yachts...

And I had promised to buy her one someday.

Guilt slammed me in the chest. Over the years, I had forgotten all the things I'd told her I would do—all the plans and dreams we'd made together. Sure, we were young with stars in our eyes and all that shit, but still...

I'd broken all my promises to her.

"You good, buddy?" Jett interrupted my thoughts. "You look like you might be sick."

"Nah, I'm good," I said, clearing my throat. "I think I'm just hungry."

"Well, good thing we're about to eat." Jett laughed and then leaned back in his chair. "It's good having you here in the flesh, you know. You really should come around more often."

"Yeah, maybe I will." *If I can make things work with Layla.*

"You know, I haven't really talked to you much," Delilah began, leaning her elbow against the table. "What kind of things do you like to do? What do you want for your future?"

*Is she for real right now?*

"Uh..." My voice trailed off as I looked to Jett for some kind of guidance. He shrugged, like *I don't know what the hell she's doing.*

"Do you want kids?" Delilah asked me when I hadn't come up with anything.

I shrugged. "I think I'd want kids. I've always said that I want them, and I don't think that's changed. I just haven't really had the opportunity, I guess."

"Would you be open to being with someone who already had kids?"

"Why the fuck are you asking me this?" I shot back at her, laughing. "That's literally the strangest question ever. Are you wanting to set me up on a blind date or something?"

"No." Delilah rolled her eyes. "I'm just trying to really get to know you, and a man who's willing to take in a woman with a child shows a lot about who they are."

"Okay, well..." I began, letting out a sigh. "I haven't ever really thought about it, because I'm not—well, I *wasn't*—interested in dating. I don't really date back in NYC. There's no point to it. But sure, if I met the right woman and she had a kid or kids, it wouldn't deter me from being with her. You can't control that stuff."

She nodded, a smile stretching across her face. "Cool, glad to hear that you're not a total douchebag. You might want to let up on the fighting though. It's only hot in the movies."

"Okay, thanks for the information." I glared at Jett, wishing he would get his wife to let up. "But for the record, I have no interest in getting into any more fights while I'm here. I won't cause either of you any problems."

"Other than the fact that you're taking time with my best friend away from me." Delilah's voice soured, though her expression didn't match, amusement dancing in her eyes.

## LUKE

"Oh, well, I'm sorry for your loss. Last time I checked the two of you live in the same town, so I'm sure you can work it out," I grunted, reaching for the water that was finally set in front of me.

"Wow, you've got an attitude," she retorted. "You might want to get that under wraps."

"Okay, okay." Jett finally shook his head. "That's enough between the two of you. Luke—" He met my gaze. "She's just being protective over Layla. That's just what she does. Don't take it personal. You should've seen the last guy Layla dated. She vetted him for nearly three hours on a double date. It was rough."

"Yeah, this is nothing compared to that asshole." Delilah made a face. "I knew he was bad news before he even showed up. All he wanted from Layla was her money, and I knew that."

My gut clenched, thinking about Layla going on a date with some guy who only wanted to use her. I had firsthand experience with gold diggers, but I hadn't ever thought about the reverse roles. "Hopefully, you ran him the fuck off after that."

"Nah." Delilah shrugged. "Layla doesn't need any help running guys off. She told him off that very night and sent him home—even paid for his ride just to get him to leave."

"I'm impressed," I said with a nod and smile, imagining Layla in a hot fit of rage. The thought turned me on, thinking of all the things she would say with my cock buried deep in her.

*What a fuckin' rush.*

"So, anyway..." Jett cleared his throat. "Just don't do anything to hurt her. I feel like she gives in to you so easily, man. She's not like that with anyone else. Like yeah, she flirts and shit, but she just melts when it comes to you."

*Nah, if that was the case, she wouldn't have left that night in NYC.*

"Whatever you say," I grunted instead. I glanced down at my watch, seeing that I only had about forty-five minutes before the conference call about the record label. "I might have to cut out if they don't show up with the food soon."

Jett raised a brow. "How come? I thought you and Layla weren't hanging out until this afternoon."

"Call with the family—I think I already mentioned it," I said with a sigh. "Jackson is fucking *determined* to get us to all pitch in together and buy the record label he's signed to. He swears he can handle the responsibility, but I don't buy it. You know how he is."

Jett shrugged. "People can change. He might be ready for something more serious."

"I think he's met someone." I glanced at my water, the thought leaving me jealous. As much as I said I didn't date, it was mostly because no one felt right...well, except for Layla.

And I still wasn't sure we could salvage that.

"Man, the thought of Jackson settling down is crazy," Jett laughed. "But cool, I'm happy for him. I hope it all works out."

"Me too." I forced a smile. "Me too."

# 19

## Layla

No matter how many miles I ran on the treadmill, nothing got rid of the heartbreak that had crept back up on me. My mind tortured me, replaying that last night with Luke over and over again. He had shut down, barely giving me any closure at all...

And then he'd fucking left the next weekend.

It had crushed my eighteen-year-old self, and while I had recovered and moved on with my life, the heartache still hurt if I thought about it too much. It made me feel crazy. Plenty of people had gotten their heart broken as teenagers and moved right past it all.

But not me.

"It's just a fling," I told myself as I stared in the mirror, having just finished blow-drying my hair. I had avoided everyone by spending all my time in the gym and then retreating to my room to get ready. It was nearly two o'clock, and no one had bothered me—not even Luke.

*Maybe he's changed his mind.*

I swallowed, hating the fact that I actually hoped he hadn't. No matter what sirens were going off in my head, I could feel myself softening to him, regardless of the past. I mean, it had been a decade ago.

As I stepped out of the bathroom, I headed to the dresser, opting for a black two-piece bathing suit. The top was strapless, though it surprisingly supported my size D boobs. The bottoms were high waisted, giving me a classic look. I grabbed a sun hat and an olive-colored cover-up that fit like a dress, cinched at the waist.

Delilah still had my book that I'd been reading, but I had an app on my phone that would have to suffice. I knew they had probably already left to go shopping and the doors connecting our rooms were locked.

A knock on the door of my room startled me as I picked up my things, shoving them all into my beach bag. My heart hammered as I headed to see who it was, and I didn't want to admit that I was hoping for a hazel-eyed hunk on the other side.

"Room service," Luke called from the other side of the door.

I rolled my eyes, ignoring the pang of excitement in my chest. "I don't think you should be trying to con your way in like that. It could get you arrested."

"Ah, you into that sort of thing? I can probably find some handcuffs." He smirked, shooting me a wink.

I shook my head and laughed as I took him in, looking more handsome than ever. He was still in the same button-up and khaki shorts, but he looked hotter than I remembered—was that even possible?

"Are you going somewhere?" he asked, eyeing the things in my hand. "I was actually thinking we could spend the afternoon on the yacht. Jett gave me permission."

My lips pursed at the idea of being alone with Luke again. "What are we going to do on the yacht?"

He gave me a devilish grin. "What do you *want* to do on the yacht?"

"You're such a man," I chided him, stepping out into the hallway. "But okay, that sounds better than lying out on the beach alone."

"Yeah, I think so. I already got the thing ready too. All that's left is you." The genuine smile on his face was the opposite of all the spite he had been shoving my way when he first got here. I didn't know what flip had been switched in him—or if it was pussy-pounding related—but my guard was up. He was already under my skin far enough as it was.

"Well, let's go on this adventure then."

The walk to the marina was short, and we spent most of it chatting about the city and the things to do there at the resort. The conversation was light and friendly, but also very shallow. It wasn't anything serious, and I made sure to focus on keeping it like that.

I needed the whole afternoon to be like that.

"Let me help you." Luke offered a hand after stepping onto the boat. "You know, I can be a gentleman."

"Do you say that so much to remind me or is that to remind yourself?" I teased, giving him a smirk as I took the offer, feeling a spark at his touch. It had always been that way between us, and it still took me by surprise.

"Ha ha," Luke retorted. "I can see that you're still going to give me all the sass, aren't you?"

"It wouldn't be right if I didn't." I dropped his hand and stepped away from him. The last thing I needed was sex on the deck of a yacht—while still in the marina for all to see.

"I'm going to go ahead and get us out a few miles, and then we can have a late lunch or early dinner," he said, giving me a proud smile. "I brought the works."

"Oh? You did, huh?"

"I did," he said with a laugh, his tan skin glistening beneath the sun. "I thought it might be nice to have a real date—not just all this hot and heavy petting."

I laughed at how ridiculous he sounded as he disappeared to steer. I knew literally *nothing* about yachts but had always loved going out on them. That was the thing about going to a rich, private school. Even though my family couldn't afford luxuries like that, all of my friends could. I'd always wanted one for myself, but...

*Yeah, never mind.*

I pushed the thought away and headed for the front, situating myself and taking a seat as the boat lurched forward. Jett had complained about it having mechanical issues time and time again, but I felt fine with it. Luke had plenty of experience when it came to boats. His dad owned one of the yacht companies, and that was where he'd gotten his start in the wealthy world.

There were clouds off in the distance, but I hadn't seen anything on the weather about a storm coming in. If anything, I would welcome the overcast skies anyway, taking a break from the scorching sun. The yacht moved with ease through the waves, and I smiled as I caught sight of dolphins swimming alongside it.

*Autumn would love this.*

I leaned over the side and, using my phone, took a quick video of the dolphins to send to Lily. The thought of my daughter's excitement made me smile as I sent the text to Lily, telling her to show Autumn. However, the moment of warmth and joy was fleeting as I thought about the human being that Luke was missing out on—her smile, her charm, and all her quirky interests. She was only five, but her personality was established.

And he was missing out on all of it.

*He doesn't want it.*

That's what I told myself over and over, but in reality, I knew that I had never even given him the option. I just hadn't felt like we would be good enough for him—and I didn't want him to just pay us off like some of the women I'd read about in similar situations.

*Yuck.*

It was about twenty minutes before Luke appeared from the cabin, having cut the engine. He was carrying a picnic basket—like, a *real* picnic basket—and I laughed as he joined me, sitting down beside me.

"I told you this was going to be legit," he teased, setting it down between us. "I didn't make the food, though. I'm no chef, but I think you already know that."

"Yeah," I giggled. "Remember the time we stayed at your parents' vacation home and you tried to make breakfast?"

"Oh god, who knew that it was possible to fuck up scrambled eggs so badly." He shook his head, a deep chuckle filling the air around us. "I have improved some since then—I can make eggs."

"Oh wow, so you are moving on up in the world." I took the sandwich he held out to me. "These look amazing," I commented as I unwrapped the thick sourdough, filled with various deli meats and veggies.

"Yeah, I found a little place off the beach that had high reviews," he said, unwrapping his own. "I made sure to tell them not to put tomatoes on yours. I know how you feel about that."

I scrunched my nose. "Yeah, I guess that's something that I haven't been able to move past."

Luke eyed me as he took a bite but didn't say anything to my comment immediately. He finished swallowing before turning to me. "So, besides hating tomatoes still, what else hasn't changed?"

There was something in his voice that made me feel like this was a shallow question with a lot of meaning, but I wasn't playing into it. I wasn't ready to go there. "I don't know. There's probably more that has changed, to be honest."

"Like you suddenly going to the gym?" He cracked a smile.

"Yeah, that," I laughed, rolling my eyes. "I don't know why I always hated the gym so much when I was younger. I guess it just reminded me too much of P.E.—and I hated that class."

"I think that's because Coach Roberts was a perv." Luke shuddered, an unpleasant look coming over his face. "You know he got fired before Jackson made it to his class."

"Oh yeah?" I nearly choked at the mention of his brother's name. Any time Luke mentioned his family, I always felt the need to bristle. While we were together, they had always been framed as the enemy...

But when I got older, I wasn't so sure.

Still, the mention of them made me uncomfortable.

"Have you listened to any of his music?" Luke took another bite but handed me a bottle of water.

"Um..." My voice trailed off as I opened it. "I have, but I wouldn't say I'm a big fan." Obviously, I wasn't going to tell him that I avoided anything that reminded me of him like the plague.

"Right," Luke chuckled. "I don't blame you. I have to say that while my brother is crazy talented, I don't listen to his music that much. It's kind of weird to listen to your brother sing about sex..."

"Ew." I scrunched up my face. "Don't point that out."

"Sorry." He eyed me. "It's just the truth."

"A very uncomfortable one. The last time I saw your brother, I don't think he was old enough to even know what sex was," I remarked, thinking of the much younger version of Jackson. It was an exaggeration, of course, but still. He was just a kid when I knew him—no rockstar, that's for sure.

"Yeah, it's been a long time. I talked to him about you recently though," Luke said casually.

I tried not to choke on the water in my mouth. "You did? I thought he had no idea who I was."

"Well..." His voice trailed off. "He always just thought you were my hot friend—which is kind of gross—but yeah."

"Oh..." The pain of the way things used to be was creeping back up on me, and I spent the next ten minutes focusing on finishing my lunch despite my waning appetite. Luke seemed to be in his own frame of mind too, and I didn't know if he'd noticed the shift, or if it was something else entirely.

"Here." He handed me an Andes Mint as he stood to his feet. "I have something I want to show you."

My heart stuttered in my chest as I nodded. "What is it?"

He gave me a sly smile. "You'll just have to see."

# 20

## Luke

I held Layla's hand as I led her to the cabin. I had gone all out for this—well, sort of. I swung open the door to the cabin, leading her to the spare bedroom on the boat. I hadn't wanted to fix up the room Jett and Delilah used because that kind of gave me the creeps.

So, I'd made it my mission to revamp the spare room.

"Oh my god..." Her voice trailed off as her hands flew to her mouth. "This is crazy."

I smiled as she took in the sight of rose petals and fake candles—I didn't think the fire hazard was worth it. "Romantic, yeah?"

She giggled, turning to me. "I'd say so."

"Too much?"

"Not at all," she laughed, though I could hear the nerves in her voice. I turned to her and reached for her cover-up, gliding it up and over her head. I had planned to ask her some questions about what she might want from us, but the throbbing dick in my pants needed to be satisfied first.

# LUKE

I held her gaze, tossing the cover-up on the floor before going for her bathing suit top. I wanted to undress her this time, and she picked up on that, letting me strip her of the top and bottom, leaving her bare.

She reached for my shirt, unbuttoning it slowly. I wanted to take over and rip it off myself, but I forced myself to let her have control, taking her sweet time. I shrugged the shirt off once she was done and stripped out of my shorts and boxer briefs.

I then pulled her to me, threading my fingers through her hair and cupping the back of her head as I brought her lips to mine. She moaned into my mouth as our naked bodies pressed to each other, skin on skin. I wanted to ravage every inch of her body, and the feeling only intensified as she began to stroke my cock, which was pressing into her lower stomach.

"I just want you to fuck me," she panted as we came up for air. "I just want you inside of me."

Her words turned me on, and I wanted to give her exactly what she wanted. I reached for the condom I had purposefully left on the bed earlier and ripped it open. She took it from me as she had before and stretched the latex over my length.

I ran my hand down her flat stomach to her pussy, growling at just how wet she already was for me. I would have no problem sliding right in, and the thought nearly brought me to my knees. Reaching around her ass, I lifted her into the air.

"*Oh!*" Layla let out a squeal, wrapping her arms around my neck. I spun us around, pinning her back against the wall as my cock pressed into her entrance. She shifted her hips, and I plunged inside of her. I had been thinking we'd have hot, sensual sex, but Layla wanted something else—and I was gonna fuck her until she was sore.

"You like this, don't you?" I growled into her ear as I held her there, my body thudding into hers.

"*Ooh*, yes," she whined, her tits bobbing with the force of my thrusts. "I want you to fuck me so hard."

"God, I love it when you talk like that," I groaned, my cock sliding easily in and out of her. Her pussy was so tight, but it was dripping with her arousal and the proof was running down my balls at the moment. "You've got the best little pussy."

She bit her lip at my words, whimpering in response as I drove into her. "I want you to fuck me from behind now."

*Man, she's in the mood to be dirty.*

I pushed us away from the wall and pulled out of her, only to spin her around and bend her over the side of the bed. I took the moment to give her ass a good hard slap, leaving behind a red handprint.

"Oh god, do it again," she moaned, wiggling her ass in front of me.

I did as she asked, popping her one more time before I spread her cheeks, giving me a full view of her glistening pussy, its swollen lips waiting for me. I lined up my cock and pressed into her. The sensation was fucking heaven as she clamped around my shaft.

"You're so tight, baby," I growled, taking my time as I worked in and out of her. Everything about this woman made my cock wanna explode, but I held back, savoring every hot, wet second I spent inside of her.

I leaned over her back, reaching to fondle her breasts while I pumped into the back of her. Our bodies slapped against each other, and she cried out with every movement, her tone sultry and lustful.

"Are you gonna cum for me?" I whispered into her ear, squeezing down on her erect nipple. "I know this drives you crazy." I squeezed a little harder as her moan increased in volume.

"*Luke*," she cried out, my name sounding like music to my ears. "I'm gonna cum."

"Cum all over my fucking cock, baby," I murmured, continuing to tease both of her nipples. I pressed her tits together, loving the feel of her flesh in my hands. Fuck, I had *always* been obsessed with her breasts, and now they were fuller and thicker than ever before.

"Oh god, oh god," she cried out as her body shivered beneath me, her orgasm pulsing around my cock. "I'm coming all over you," she whined, just before moaning out my name in a way that nearly drove me right over the edge...but I held it together. If we were being dirty, I wanted my cum all over those tits.

I fucked her pussy until she had come down, her body sagging beneath me. Then, I pulled out of her. "Turn around and climb onto the bed," I instructed her, gesturing to the rose-petal-covered bed.

With a gleam in her eye, she did as I said, climbing up and rolling onto her back. She held my gaze as I straddled her torso, positioning my dick between her tits. She did me the favor of pulling the condom off, already knowing what I wanted.

"You're such a good girl," I praised her as she tossed it off to the side. "You know I want those tits to make me cum."

"Yes," she moaned, grabbing them. She pressed them against my length, bouncing them up and down as I thrust with my hips. "You like this?" Layla eyed me, her green eyes dark with lust.

"Fuck yes I do," I growled. "Your tits are perfect, baby. They're fucking perfect."

"Ooh," she moaned, squeezing them together even tighter. I let out a groan as she did so, feeling the excitement come to a head in my body.

I tensed, meeting her gaze. "I'm gonna spew my cum all over them." I pulled my dick out from in between them just in time for my climax, pleasure rattling my entire body as I shot hot liquid all over her creamy skin. It was fucking perfect, and when I was done, I leaned down, pressing a kiss to her lips.

"Stay there," I said, my voice still strained with lust. "I'll clean you up."

She nodded, lying still as I disappeared into the bathroom, grabbing a towel and getting it damp in the sink. I returned with a smile on my face, cleaning her up in both places.

"I swear, you're the most beautiful woman I've ever met," I murmured as I tossed the towel onto the floor.

She sat up, giving me a lopsided smile. "You always used to say that."

"Yeah." I nodded. "And I always meant it when I said it too."

She didn't say anything, sliding off the bed and grabbing for her bathing suit. I went for my boxer briefs, realizing that this was not going to lead to any pillow talk like I'd hoped for.

"Why are you always in a rush?" I asked her once my shorts were buttoned. "We used to lie in bed naked for hours after sex."

She eyed me with a weird expression on her face. "You know you're referring to a *decade* ago, right? Like, that was before I grew up and out of that habit."

"Can I ask you something?" The question came out before I could rethink what I was about to say.

"Sure." She sat back down on the bed, looking up at me. "What's up?"

"Why'd you cut out in the middle of the night in New York? I thought the whole thing had gone well...and then I woke up and you were just...*gone.*" The moment of vulnerability was not something I was comfortable remembering, but I *needed* to know why she'd left me like that.

"Um..." Her voice trailed off like I had caught her off guard. "I guess...well..."

"Like, did I do something wrong? Because I fucking replayed that night over and over in my head for months, Layla. I couldn't let it go and I couldn't come up with a good reason as to why you left. Well, other than—"

"It's not what you think," she cut me off, shaking her head and letting out a sigh. "It's just...that was the first time I had seen you since you broke up with me before college, and all I could think about was that I didn't want a repeat of it. Our relationship had always been hidden...and I had friends who were waiting on me too," she added quickly, diverting her gaze from mine.

"We could've talked about it over breakfast or something," I said quietly, taking a seat beside her, though I left a good foot between us. "I could've done a lot of things, and I thought that night might've led to something more."

She made a face at me, her eyes filling with confusion. "We were drunk, Luke. And the fact that we ran into each other was a crazy coincidence. Like, the city is *huge*, and somehow we still bumped into each other that night."

"I wasn't that drunk, Layla," I commented, unable to let go of the deflection. "And you weren't either. We left after two fucking drinks. I don't think that counts."

"Okay, so maybe I just...I've never been...I hadn't started my company then, you know? I was still trying to figure things out. I wasn't in that much different of a place than I had been when you broke up with me before college."

"Why did it matter what place you were in?" I questioned, shaking my head at her. "Were you just in the middle of trying to start it and too busy for a relationship or something?"

She went quiet and the look on her face made me think I was missing the point. "Uh, I hadn't even thought of the company at that point, Luke. I was still just trying to figure out my place in the world, I guess."

"Okay, but..." My voice trailed off as I searched her face. "I still don't get what that has to do with you running out? We were together when neither of us knew what the fuck we were going to do in life—well, other than each other," I added with a laugh.

She didn't laugh. "I seriously just don't think you understand what I'm trying to say, Luke. Like, it's not like—"

A crack of thunder cut her off before she could finish, and her eyes went wide at the sound above us. "Is that...?"

"What the hell?" I turned to the door, racing toward the stairs to the deck. No one had warned me about a storm...but it looked like mother nature was taking over our outing.

# 21

## Layla

I ran after Luke, my footsteps clumsy as I trotted up the stairs to the deck, nearly landing on my face a couple of times. My head was a wreck from everything, and I knew I was falling for Luke again.

Well, or maybe I wasn't *falling*—I was just coming to terms with the fact that maybe my feelings for him were more genuine than nostalgic.

And that was terrifying.

"Holy shit..." Luke gasped, standing outside on the deck. "That's a monster."

I shoved the door the rest of the way open, my jaw dropping at the change in temperature—and the disappearance of the sun. The boat rocked, and I lost my footing, falling into Luke's back. I caught myself, and he turned to help me, his arms wrapping around my waist.

Once somewhat steady, I cast my gaze in the direction Luke had been looking, and my heart dropped at the dark skies and massive cumulonimbus clouds. I was no meteorologist, but from what little I did know, it looked intimidating…

And then as I turned my head to take in our surroundings, my heart flip-flopped in my chest. "Um, Luke…I think…I think we've drifted." There was no shore in view…and there were no other boats either.

He was still gripping my waist—and the metal handle just outside the door. "Yeah, I know we've drifted, but we shouldn't have drifted too far…I don't think. I don't know. I was so focused on the motor not starting that I didn't look at our location. Either way, it still won't take us long to get back…and we can outrun that." He gestured to the impending storm. "Let's get back inside. No need to be out here on the deck, and these waves are only going to get worse."

"*Great*," I muttered, letting him lead the way back to the door, holding me steady.

"Yeah, we just need to get back to shore…" His voice was strained as a gust of cool wind slammed into us. "Might be a gnarly storm. We should probably call someone at the shore and see what they say about it."

I nodded, the realization hitting me that my uneven steps up the stairs had been because of the growing waves. "I-I'll call Delilah."

"Probably not a bad idea," Luke agreed, the two of us hustling. I grabbed my phone from the spare room and joined Luke in the cockpit. I hit the unlock button, my heart dropping as I saw that only twenty percent of my battery life was left.

*I need to find a charger on this thing.*

But first, I needed to call Delilah. I pulled up her contact information and hit the call button beside her name, putting the call on speaker.

# LAYLA

Luke wasn't paying much attention, a serious look on his face as he tried to start the motor—which, after a few seconds of watching, I suddenly realized was *not* starting.

"Hey, I bet you're calling about the storm rolling in," Jett answered instead of my best friend, a chuckle following his words. "It's apparently quite a storm. You'll probably wanna head in. They're saying the winds are gonna be crazy, and you know what that means—killer waves."

"Yeah, and we'd be heading in, but the boat won't start," Luke called over his shoulder as he kept working on it.

"Why'd you turn it off?" Jett's voice dropped with concern. "Man, it's a finicky piece of shit. You might have to bypass the starter...I don't know. It's hard to say. I might be able to walk you through it if you need me to." The boat lurched to the left, and I nearly fell over, catching myself on the wall. The phone thudded to the floor, and Luke swept it up.

"Okay, tell me how to start this boat," he demanded, taking Jett off speaker and putting the phone up to his ear.

My stomach knotted up for more reasons than just the storm as he held my phone. All it would take was for him to exit out of the phone call and he would see a picture of Autumn...and then we'd *really* have a storm on our hands. At the same time, I couldn't help but admire his strong jawline, and the stubble beginning to show. His face was tense while he concentrated, trying different ways to emergency start the boat...

Which was now being thrown to the right.

I braced myself against the wall as a strong wave of nausea surged through my body from the movement. I'd never been one to get seasick, but then again, I couldn't remember the last time I'd been caught in a storm either. I'd only ever been out with Jett and Delilah in calm waters—and with Luke when we were younger. I shut my eyes and tried to take deep breaths as bile rose in my throat. I heard the engine sputter...and then die.

Over and over again.

*We're going to be stuck out here.*

Luke's voice was growing more frantic as he left me there, heading out of the room. "I'll be right back," he said to me, giving me a half-hearted smile before continuing to speak in a low voice into the phone.

*Please get us back to the marina.*

The skies were darkening, and the waves were growing in size, the sight frightening as I peered out the window of the cockpit. I took a seat in one of the chairs and braced myself as the first large splatters of rain crashed into the glass.

*It's just a storm. People ride them out all the time.*

But as I told myself it was no big deal...

It *felt* like a big deal.

The few raindrops turned to buckets of water within seconds, and the yacht took another hard plunge to the left, sending me tumbling out of the chair. A sharp pain seared through my wrist, and I tried to shake it out, wincing as I did. My mind started pulling up images of all the times I had seen boats capsizing on the news, and I shuddered, fear pulsing through my body.

I glanced back toward the door where Luke had left, tuning my ear to the engine, but not hearing anything. I had no idea about boats and motors, but I did know there was a room with a lot of the mechanical and electrical components of the boat—and that was probably where he had gone. I scooted myself across the floor, placing my back firmly against the wall. This was a multimillion-dollar super yacht, and for all the luxuries it had, it was *seriously* lacking in the way of being reliable, apparently.

*I'll never set foot on this boat again.*

Wrapping my arms around myself, I wished that Luke would've taken his own phone instead of mine. I needed some sort of distraction from the way we were being thrown around. A crack of thunder sent me jumping sideways, and I shook my head, chiding myself for being such a wimp. Jett and Luke had both told stories about being caught in storms on their yachts, and honestly, Luke had tons of experience with these boats. I was in good hands.

"I don't know what the fuck to do then." Luke's voice grabbed my attention as he reappeared. "I wish you would've told me there was a chance it would lock up like that." His face was contorted with concern, lines forming around his eyes as he shook his head, going back to the control panel.

"No luck?" I asked, my voice sheepish as I looked up at him.

He glanced down at me, giving me a weird look—probably because I was sitting on the floor—and then shook his head. "No luck, and we might have to ride out what's coming."

I did *not* like the sound of that. "There's no way to get it started?"

"Looks like the motor is finally locked up," Luke grunted, talking to me and into the phone. "I think you should find a new mechanic." Whatever Jett said to him made him laugh, though it wasn't bright and deep like usual. "Yeah, okay. Well, let me see where we are."

My bare foot tapped anxiously on the floor as I watched him peer at the GPS navigation screen. He squinted at it for a few moments.

"Jeez, we really drifted," Luke groaned.

I pulled my knees to my chest and dropped my head to my knees, my stomach rolling again as we were slung around. Luke balanced himself through it, continuing to talk to Jett about our location—which was apparently much further out than he initially thought.

*How did we drift so far?*

Before I could really contemplate the question, I jumped to my feet, rushing toward the nearest bathroom. I slung the door open and dove for the toilet, barely making it before I vomited, losing what I had eaten earlier.

*Ugh.*

I didn't stop until I had lost all the contents of my stomach, and even then, I still felt woozy. Working to keep myself steady, I cleaned myself up and flung open the medicine cabinet above the sink. I dug through the contents, letting out a sigh of relief as I saw Dramamine.

"Oh, thank god," I mumbled, ripping open the brand-new box and taking the medicine. I leaned against the sink, shutting my eyes as I waited, hoping it would work faster than ever.

"Layla?" Luke's voice called from the other side of the door. "Are you okay?"

"Just seasick," I called back. "I found the Dramamine in the cabinet though—all good."

"Okay..." His voice trailed off. "It's probably a good idea to take it. It's only going to get worse."

*Great. Fucking great.*

"Okay, do you want some?"

"Nah, I'm good. I've been riding out storms since I was a kid. It's never bothered my stomach."

I reached for the door, opening it to see Luke standing just outside, his face a little less stressed than it was before. "So, I take it the boat isn't going to start?"

He shook his head. "Nope, I don't think so. I think the motor is finally shot, so we're gonna be stuck to ride this out. No need to go

# LAYLA

calling the coast guard. We'll be fine. Jett said from what he can tell on the weather, it's not nearly as bad as it looks. He is gonna call his mechanic to see if there's anything else we can try."

I nodded, trying not to show how panicked I felt inside. My eyes flickered to my phone in his left hand. "Can I have my phone back?"

"Oh yeah, sure," he said with a smile, holding it out to me. "You might wanna charge it though. Also, Jett might come back on. He's just on hold while he calls the mechanic."

"Okay," I muttered, the sound of the storm startling as I stepped back out into the small captain's lounge area outside the cockpit. I followed him shakily back to the cockpit, glancing down at the call on hold.

"I'll grab you a phone charger," Luke called, heading off toward one of the rooms. "I saw one earlier."

"Thanks." I made my way back to the spot where I'd been just before I'd thrown up, sliding back down to the floor. I didn't know what it was about the floor, but it felt better than trying to balance in the chair.

"Here." Luke reappeared, plugging the charger into the wall for me and handing me the charging end. "The generator is still working, so we shouldn't be without electricity."

"Great," I forced out as I plugged my phone in.

"You there?" Jett's voice came over the speaker.

"Yeah," Luke and I said in unison.

"There's nothing more you can do to get it running. You'll have to ride it out and wait on a tow." Jett's voice sounded grave. "You sure you don't wanna put it in to the coast guard?"

"I'll keep an eye on it, but so far the waters are mild. I've dropped the anchor to keep us right with the storm."

*Mild?*

I held in my groan. *Nothing* about the way we were getting tossed around felt *mild*.

Jett laughed. "Best of luck to you. Enjoy the ride."

# 22

## Luke

"It's just a thunderstorm, not a hurricane," I said to Layla, giving her a reassuring smile. As much as I hated to admit it, I was more concerned about how far we had drifted *before* the storm than the storm itself. I wasn't sure how long it would be before someone came to the rescue. Overall, my concern was low. Based on everything Jett had found on the weather, it might get a little rough, but it really was a mild storm...

However, the look on Layla's face told me she wasn't finding any comfort in my words.

"How long will it last?" She looked up at me, her eyes wide and laced with fear.

"I don't know," I said with a sigh. "Based on the size of the storm...maybe a couple of hours? It's not as scary as it looks."

Layla nodded, dropping her face to her phone. She was confined to the reach of the charger plugged into the wall, and I watched as she typed out what I would assume to be a long text.

*She's probably telling Delilah how awful I am for taking her out in this.*

I tried to push away the guilt and frustration of turning what I'd hoped to be the start of a second chance into a terrifying experience for her. "I'm gonna go grab my phone," I muttered, heading to the spare room. "I won't be gone long."

"Okay," she replied, her eyes never leaving the screen.

The cell service had disappeared, but the boat's Wi-Fi was still working—for now, anyway. Jett said the batteries were weak, and the generator wasn't great either. So basically, we had shit chances of keeping the luxuries going. *That* was something I wasn't going to tell Layla yet.

I grabbed my phone from inside the nightstand, groaning as I saw the texts and missed calls from Jackson.

*Call me.*

*Dude! Call me!*

*Come on... Don't ignore me!*

I rolled my eyes, not surprised by my brother's inability to realize that the world didn't revolve around him. I scrolled through the texts and checked that my Wi-Fi calling was enabled before putting the phone to my ear.

"Luke! What the hell, man? I've been calling for hours." Jackson sounded irritated and not the least bit concerned about my well-being.

A crack of thunder rolled in the background and the ship dove hard to the right, but stayed straight, so I wasn't concerned. Without the motor, I couldn't power through the squall, so it was all I could do to just keep us at the right angle.

"Sorry, caught in a storm on a yacht with no motor," I said, balancing with one hand against the wall. "What's up?"

# LUKE

He was silent for a second. "Why the hell are you on a yacht with no motor?"

"Great question," I retorted, ignoring the roll in my stomach. That was how I dealt with seasickness—just ignore it until it goes away. "Jett's mechanic is probably to blame, or this lemon of a rig. I think it needs to be scrapped."

"Obviously," Jackson snorted. "Must not be too bad of a storm if you're making phone calls."

"Yeah, it's mild, really," I answered, shrugging my shoulders. "A little loud, but mild. Layla's not so sure about what to make of it, though. I think it's freaking her out."

"Must be her first one," Jackson chuckled.

"It is, I think." I headed back to the cockpit, thankful that I'd spent half my life on boats. It was second nature, considering my family owned multiple boat manufacturers—though thankfully not the maker of *this* specific yacht.

"So, how much longer in Miami? We all need to meet about this label. I was hoping we could get together tomorrow."

"*What*?" I snapped. "I told you I'll be here for another two weeks."

"Oh, come on, just take a couple days and meet with us in New York City."

"If I fly back to the city, I'm not coming back to Miami," I warned, though I knew that was a little dramatic. If Layla was still in Miami, I would more than likely come back on whim and not even think twice about it.

"We'll come to you then," Jackson said, his voice matter-of-fact. "Dad is flying in this evening, so it would be no big deal for us to just take the jet to Miami."

I let out a heavy sigh, running a hand over my face. "Why is this such a freaking rush, Jack? Can it seriously not wait until I'm back in the city?"

"*No*, there's another offer being made, and they want to make a decision before the end of the weekend."

"They're being that stubborn?" I shook my head, not surprised by the antics of the sellers. They were playing a hard game to see who was serious about it—and more than likely, they didn't think that Jackson was serious.

"Dude, I want this so bad," Jackson urged. "But we need your expertise too. You're great at going over financials and the final negotiation. You're even better than Dad."

"Okay, okay," I said with a sigh. "Sure, I can meet you tomorrow..." My voice trailed off as I watched Layla from afar, staring out the window as the storm battered the yacht. "I think we'll be in by tomorrow."

"Call the coast guard," Jackson said in my ear. "You know it's not worth it to be stuck out there without power. It sucks."

*Unless you're stuck with someone you love.*

"Yeah, I don't want to bother the coast guard right now," I said, cautious with my tone. "I'm sure they're busy with other more pressing matters in the middle of this pop-up storm. There're people in much worse shape."

"I don't know how it could be much worse than not having a motor, Luke," Jackson chuckled. "But it's whatever you wanna do, man. You're the one who spent all that time on boats growing up, not me."

"Yeah, I think I can handle it," I laughed, shaking my head. "Just let me know when you guys fly in. Are you gonna stay in one of the condos?"

"Probably, I don't know though. I have a buddy that's got a place right off the beach. I think we'll just go there if I can talk him into it."

"Right, sounds good," I said, my voice blank as Layla glanced over to me, a curious expression on her face. "I'll let you know when we make it to shore."

"Okey dokey," Jackson said. "Call the coast guard if it gets bad."

"Yep." With that, I hung up the phone, shoving it back into my pocket. As long as the yacht could maintain the Wi-Fi, we'd have plenty of entertainment. The storm wouldn't be roaring forever, and as I made my way to the cockpit to join Layla, I could already see that we were through the roughest part…

Though she still didn't look relieved in the slightest.

"It's not so bad," I said to her, taking a seat in the captain's chair. "It could be a lot worse."

"I guess," she let out a heavy sigh, before going back to her phone.

"Who are you talking to?" I tried to sound nonchalant, but she gave me a weird look regardless. I shrugged, hoping to loosen the growing tension. Everything had felt mostly perfect…until this fiasco.

"I'm just talking to my sister," Layla muttered, her voice quiet and almost sheepish.

"I promise that we're gonna be fine." I knew I was basically repeating myself over and over, but I just wanted her to *believe* it. "There's nothing to be scared of."

Her lips pursed as she once again met my gaze. "But what if…" Her voice trailed off as if she wasn't sure she wanted to ask me the question. "What if we get lost at sea?"

I raised my brows, trying not to chuckle. "We're not going to get lost at sea. This yacht isn't going to sink or something in a mild storm like this. Storms are a little spooky"—I glanced to the rain pummeling the windows—"but we have emergency backup power, and I have a satellite phone and GPS. There's nothing to worry about—other than the bill of having to be towed back to the marina."

She smiled, though it didn't reach her eyes. "If you say so."

I grabbed onto the seat as we took another dive. It was crazy riding out a storm, you could drop the equivalent of five to ten flights of stairs in a matter of seconds. "One time," I began, the thought sparking a memory, "I was out with my dad—it was a few years ago—and there was a big tropical storm coming in. We had gone out to go deep sea fishing, and we pushed our luck out on the water, catching part of the storm. The boat dropped so far that it made my ears pop from the quick altitude change."

"That doesn't make me feel any better," she said, though she let out a little laugh. "This isn't like that storm though, is it?"

"Oh, hell no," I laughed. "It's not any fun to sit here and ride the waves like this, since we don't have a motor right now, but it's not really *that* dangerous. It would take something pretty nasty...and if that were the case, I would call the coast guard for rescue."

Just as the words left my mouth, a mayday call came over the radio, sending Layla's eyes wide open. I listened to the coordinates of the small fishing boat, comparing them to our own.

"Three miles away—toward the shore," I said, my heart picking up its pace, wishing that we could offer assistance. Thankfully, within just a few seconds, another boat came over the radio, letting them know they'd be there in about five minutes, being less than half a mile away. However, that didn't serve to help Layla's fear, and I reached for her hand as she visibly trembled.

"I promise, everything is okay," I said softly, pulling her into my lap. She leaned into me, her head resting against my shoulder as the boat swayed. I breathed in the scent of her hair, and while I knew the moment was scary for her, I was committing it to memory for me.

Fuck, I'd missed the way it felt to be needed.

And that was something I hadn't felt in the longest time. No one had needed me in the way that Layla had always made me feel she did. I kept my arms around her, keeping my eyes on the waves. I fought the urge to tell her the way I felt—the way I wanted a second chance—but instead held back. The last thing I wanted was to ruin it.

"It's almost passed," I murmured into her ear, and she squeezed me a little tighter. "It won't be long, and it'll be gone, nothing but clear skies ahead," I added, just as there was another clap of thunder around us. "Then we can go back to enjoying the evening."

*And waiting for rescue and a tow back to the marina...*

However long that would take.

# 23

## Layla

I latched onto Luke and didn't let go until the storm had passed in its entirety, the evening sun streaming through the window. Something about letting him hold me was nearly healing, though it was hard to put my finger on *why* that was. After all, it felt almost like a betrayal of my heart to let the man who had shattered me all those years ago back in. I wanted to keep my guard up—I *needed* to keep my guard up. This was just a fling—at best...

Though I had to admit the effort he was putting in seemed a lot more than that.

"It's gone now," Luke said softly in my ear, his hot breath tickling my skin. "I need to make sure it didn't move us too far."

"Okay," I said, forcing myself away from him. I didn't want to move, and honestly, the part of me that wanted to stay there forever with him was starting to become more and more dominant. I stood shakily to my feet, Luke offering a hand as he stood to his feet as well, taking in our location on the navigation system.

"Shit," he muttered, shaking his head. "We just keep drifting further out."

I chewed my lip, trying not to worry. "But they can still come and get us, right?"

"Yeah, it just might be a while," Luke said, his eyes not moving from the screen. He pulled out his cell phone, typing quickly and then taking a picture of a screen. "I think it's time to make the call for a tow."

My eyes widened. "You haven't already done that? I thought we were just having to wait until the storm passed for them to leave and get us."

"It's fine, Layla," he shot back at me, his voice a little irritated. "I promise you that nothing is going to happen to us. There's enough food on this thing for *days*. We're not in dire need of a rescue or something. It's all fine."

"Okay, sorry," I muttered, shrugging my shoulders as I backed away from him. Now that the waters were calmer, I decided to let him be and take care of the calls he needed to make to get us out of here. I slipped away into the lounge, pulling my phone out of my pocket. I smiled as I saw a text from Delilah.

*Did you survive the storm? It's raining like crazy here. I think I might melt.*

I opened the door into the stairwell, slipping out onto the deck. The air was still cooler than it had been before the storm had rolled in, but the sun was shining, warming my face. I wandered out to the railing, peering out as far as I could see, and what I could see...

Was nothing but ocean.

I had been out this far before, though it was only a handful of times. There was something beautiful about it, and the haze left by the storm left the skies a striking shade of orange, the sun illuminating them. I sent Delilah a text to let her know that I was still living and breathing—and that the storm had passed.

I just hoped we wouldn't drift further out while we waited for rescue. My phone pinged again in my hand, and I glanced down at it, expecting to either see a text from Delilah or Lily. I had checked in with Autumn in the middle of the storm. It was Delilah.

*Jett's going with the crew to get the yacht.*

I liked the text from her, feeling more relieved that they would be heading out to get us soon.

"Hey." Luke's voice came from behind me, and I turned to see him, a smile on his face. "I was wondering where you took off to."

"I was just seeing what everything was like after the storm."

"Beautiful, isn't it?" He gestured to the skies that I had just been admiring. "Almost as beautiful as you." Luke winked, grabbing my hand and pulling me into him.

"You're too sweet," I teased him, thankful that his snippy tone was long gone. I knew that he was just taking care of everything, and I was probably annoying him with my worries.

"Not as sweet as you taste," he murmured, taking my mouth with his. His tongue slipped between my lips, stroking mine as his hands traveled down my waist, slipping underneath the bottom of my cover-up. I let out a moan as he gave my ass a tight squeeze, and he broke his lips from mine.

"We still have some time before they get here, you know," Luke said, his tone husky as he kissed my jaw between words. "And I've always wanted to fuck you out here in the open. No one will see."

I giggled, my thighs clenching as his hands dropped lower, teasing around the hem of my bathing suit bottoms. "I dare you to," I murmured, pulling away to meet his gaze.

"Mmm, I like that challenge." He chuckled darkly, before spinning me around and pressing his hard cock into my backside. His hands roamed over my body, both coming to a stop at my chest. He squeezed my breasts, stoking the ache building in my pussy. I wanted him to bend me right over the rail and fuck me, but at the same time, I was happy for him to take his time.

He moved my hair to the side, kissing the side of my neck as his hands untied my cover-up, backing away just enough to let it fall to the deck. He growled in satisfaction, running his fingertips over my bare stomach.

"You're so fucking perfect," he muttered, one hand slipping up and under my top, finding my erect nipple. He gave it a light squeeze, and I cried out, my pussy growing wet at the touch. His other hand finally slid underneath my bikini bottoms, sliding across my pelvis before slipping into my folds. "And you're so wet for me. You're always so ready for me."

"Mmm," I moaned as he rubbed my clit, working circles around it. I ground my ass into his cock, loving the way it felt against my backside. I knew what was there underneath, and my body wanted to wrap around his cock, lodging it deep inside of me.

As if he understood my needs, he slid two fingers into my pussy, moving slow at first. My head tipped back, resting against his chest. Two fingers inside of me, and his other hand palming my breasts, my arousal began to build as I squirmed against him.

"You're such a good girl," he whispered in my ear, just before nibbling on my earlobe. "So fucking sexy."

"*Ooh*," I cried, my sultry tone growing. We were in the middle of the ocean, and there was no way anyone was going to hear... "*Luke*!" My volume increased as his hand began to work faster, and his fingers pinched my erect nipple.

"I want you to cum for me like this," he growled. "And then cum again around my cock."

I nodded, my breath increasing as I reached the peak, my pussy exploding with my orgasm. I clenched around his fingers, and he growled in satisfaction.

"Just like that, baby," he groaned, pressing his cock into my back. "Just like that. You cum so good."

My eyes squeezed shut as I rode out the pleasure until the very end, Luke's fingers not pulling out until I had completely come down from the high I was on. I spun around to face him, and he caught my lips in a hot and heady kiss. My fingers unsnapped his shorts, letting them drop to the deck floor, his erection bouncing free against my stomach.

I stroked his length, and he groaned at the contact, his kiss growing more and more desperate with every passing second. He untied the string on the back of my bikini, and my tits fell free, pressing against his chest. Luke then shoved my bottoms down, the ocean breeze hitting my bare body.

We stroked each other before he reached down, picking me up from the deck. I wrapped my legs around him, grinding my wet pussy up and down his cock the best I could. I wanted him inside of me, and he carried me until he laid me down on one of the exterior lounge couches, still damp from the storm.

He situated himself between my legs, and for the first time in a long time, I was thankful I was on birth control. He ran the tip of his dick along my entrance, wetting it with my natural lubrication.

"Your pussy is so perfect," he growled, pressing into me an inch or so. "And so fucking *tight*. Tell me how good I feel, baby."

"You feel so good," I whimpered as he pressed into me further, my body stretching to take his thick girth. No matter how many times he fucked me, it was always an experience fitting him inside of me. "I want you so bad." The words left my lips before I could stop them.

"I want you too," he murmured, meeting my gaze. "I missed you so much."

Emotions swelled in my chest, and I struggled not to say more than I should, instead pulling his lips to mine. I kissed him to shut myself up, and he groaned with want as he finally pressed himself all the way into me. I cried out at the way he filled me entirely.

His hands gripped my ass, holding me against the wall as he thrust into me over and over, his lips devouring me. All I could feel was Luke, and I didn't mind if he kept me pinned to the wall of the yacht for hours. He fucked me, his cock hitting just the right spot inside of me, and my second orgasm began to build.

"*Oh,* just like that!" I cried out, breaking away from him long enough to spit the words out and take a long, deep breath, my lungs desperate for air.

"You feel so good," he groaned, his own body tensing against me. "I'm gonna cum."

I cried out his name right as the orgasm ravaged my body, clenching down on his cock. He gasped out at the sensation, his body following in pursuit. He came hard, growling into my neck as he stilled against me, the weight of him still pinning me against the wall. Once we had both come down from the ecstasy, he pulled away, planting a soft kiss on my lips.

Neither of us said anything as he pulled out of me, letting me drop to my feet. Instead of immediately walking away to get dressed, I grabbed for him, standing on my tiptoes and planting one last kiss on his cheek.

"This has been a good day," I said softly, my words inciting surprise on his face.

"Even with a dead motor and the storm? I figured I might've ruined any shot at a second chance with you, honestly." His words were a little shocking, considering I hadn't been expecting them to come out of his mouth...ever. I didn't know why, but I never thought that he would *actually* want that...from me, anyway.

"We've always had something special," I said to him, giving him a smile before going for my clothes a few feet away. "It's hard to ignore the connection that we have."

"Yeah, and it's crazy," Luke admitted, grabbing up his shorts and slipping into them. "It's like no matter how much time passes between us, there's always something there… I think it'll always be there, Layla."

I stopped, swallowing the lump growing in my throat. "You really think so?"

His entire face softened, showing a side I hadn't seen from him in years. "Yeah, I really do think so."

I nodded, my heart swelling in my chest. *Maybe we could have a second chance.*

# 24

## Luke

I fought the urge to stare at Layla as she ate a sandwich, hours having passed since I called for a tow back to the marina. Jett was determined to tag along, which might have been why it was taking longer than usual...but I had to admit, the time alone with Layla as a result wasn't so bad. She was in a good mood, and I didn't really want the time to end.

"So, you're going to buy a record label, huh?" She laughed, setting the sandwich down on the table. It was dark out now, but we had hidden away in the captain's lounge. I wanted to stay as close to the navigation system as possible. Granted, I wasn't sure how long we'd have power...

"Yeah, I guess I'm going to buy a record label with my brothers and dad," I said, pushing away the increasing worry about the power. "I think it's a good investment...not one that I would've chosen on my own, but you know."

She nodded. "I guess that's good though. I think it would be cool to own a record label."

"Yeah, well, I'll happily take you along if you want to see the place?" I offered, hoping Layla would take me up on it. I knew it sounded crazy, but any hope she would give me that this would last beyond the vacation made me feel like there was a chance I might get to have her again for real...

And I wouldn't let her go if I did.

She smiled. "That would be fun. I bet you'll get to hear a lot of different artists."

"Yeah, probably so." Just as I got the words out, my phone started to ring, and I dug it out of my pocket, hoping it would be Jett. Much to my dismay, it was not...

"Hey, Jackson," I answered, standing up from the table to speak to him in private. "I take it you know when you'll be here?"

"No..." Jackson's voice trailed off. "Actually, I was calling to make sure you're okay. I got a friend down there that said the storm caused two shipwrecks. I just wanted to make sure you weren't one of them."

"No," I said, a little surprised by the news. "I heard the mayday for one of the boats, but there was another boat close. I figured they were fine. Where was the second?"

"I don't know the specifics right now. Marty, one of my bandmates, is down there and told me. I was worried it might've been you, since you didn't have any power."

"Nah, not us," I said, running my fingers through my hair and slipping away as I caught Layla's concerned looks. I didn't want her to worry. "So was everyone okay? Do you know?"

He was silent. "It says the search for a couple of people is still ongoing." His voice was quiet. "It kind of freaked me out, to be honest. I was thinking about you, and for some reason, I just *knew* it was you.

I'm glad it's not though. My anxiety is a real shitty quality sometimes. I always go thinking about the worst-case scenario."

"Yeah, well, it happens to the best of us. We're still out here though," I added, wondering if the rescues were the reason that we hadn't been towed in yet. "I don't know how much longer we'll have to wait, either—or how long these damn batteries will last. There was a backup generator on here, but something shorted. It doesn't look to be functioning. I haven't told Layla that yet."

"Oh shit, man," he sounded concerned. "The last thing you want is to go dark."

"I know that," I snapped, my worry heightening. Jackson never worried about anything, so the fact that he was worried stressed me out. "I have a satellite phone here. I just might not have a navigation system. They'll have to try and find us."

"That's fucking stressful. You want me to call some of the connections I have? I bet Dad's got some connections too."

*Why didn't I think of that?*

Shaking my head at myself, I peeked out Layla, who was now on her phone. "I think I'm going to give Dad a call. Now is a good time to take him up on those connections."

"Yeah, I agree," Jackson said. "Be safe. Love ya."

The last two words caught me off guard, but I appreciated them, nonetheless. "Love ya too, man." I hung up the phone and quickly scrolled to my dad's number, hoping he would answer.

"Hey, Luke," he answered. "Jackson told me you got stranded on Jett's yacht. I told ya he should've bought one of ours."

"Yeah, yeah, I know," I chuckled, not surprised by his words. He clearly hadn't been keeping up with news of the other boats having wrecked. "I take it you know that the engine is dead too, right?"

"Well, that's what Jackson said, but he didn't give me any specifics. I just landed in New York City, so I haven't had much time to check in with him."

"Yeah, okay," I said, nodding. "Well, it's locked up, and uh, I don't know how much life we have left before we lose power. I really need a tow back to the marina. We've drifted a long way out..."

"How far out? Ten miles?"

"No, no, more like fifty, I think. I don't know, I've been sharing my location with Jett. I don't know what's taking him so long to get out here. I know there's been a couple shipwrecks, and one of those is in the middle of a search and rescue..."

"Oh shit, son." My dad's voice dropped. "Did the boat take any damage?"

"I don't think so. I think we didn't take the storm head-on, luckily. It must've shifted or something."

"That's good." He breathed out a heavy sigh. "I think I got a buddy who might be able to get out there to tow you in. I don't know how busy he is—or if he's even in Miami right now."

"That would be really freaking awesome," I admitted, feeling a little relieved. "I don't want to be stuck out here all night."

"Be mindful of power," he instructed me. "You got emergency lights or a backup?"

"I don't know. I guess I need to check that," I said, running my fingers through my hair. "I'm not gonna lie, I expected them to come and tow us a lot sooner than this. I don't understand why it's taking so long."

"I don't know," Dad replied. "There could be a million reasons, and I wouldn't know a single one of them. You're just gonna have to hang tight. Like I said, I can make some calls. If Dave can't get out there to you, I'm sure he'll know someone who can. Once I round up Jackson and Eli, we're gonna head down there. Hopefully, you'll be back in by then."

I shrugged. "I sure as hell hope so. Losing power would be a fucking nightmare. It will freak Layla out too."

"Layla?" Dad questioned, a tone of surprise in his voice. "Who's Layla? Are you talking about your old friend from high school?"

I hesitated, a knot growing in my stomach. "Yeah, that's the one. Layla Miller is her full name. She's best friends with Jett's wife, Delilah."

"Man, it's been a long time since I heard her name. I always thought you were gonna end up dating her, but you never did. It really surprised me."

"Yeah..." My voice trailed off, not even knowing what to say to that—until my mother came to my mind. "Mom would've killed me if I had dated her. She only went to the school because her mom was a teacher there."

"She definitely would've," he scoffed, his voice growing sour. "But I don't think you should let her opinion about anything bother you now. I don't even know where she is, anymore. She met that Italian guy, started a new family, and has basically just dropped off the face of the earth."

"Oh? So she's got a new man, again?" I shifted uncomfortably. I hated discussing my mom...especially with my dad. Even all these years later, he still seemed a little sour about it all—and I couldn't blame him for it. She had left a deep wound that I wasn't sure would ever heal completely.

"Yeah, but anyway..." He cleared his throat. "I'll let you go, so I can make a few calls. If you wouldn't mind, send me your location so I can send it to Dave. I'm sure I can get a few people moving in your favor."

"Thanks, Dad." I breathed out a sigh of relief. "Let me know what you find out, so I can get ready."

"Yeah, well, in the meantime, you figure out what to do if you run out of power."

"Yes, sir," I quipped before hanging up. I hesitated before joining Layla, hearing her laughing on the phone. I didn't want to break the news that we might run out of power before we were rescued. It would scare her, because the dangers of having no lights were more frightening to me than the actual storm.

Before heading back out, I dialed Jett's phone, hoping he had an update on when he would be out to come and get us. It rang four times before he finally picked it up.

"I'm working on it," he said, his tone full of defeat. "Apparently, there's barely anyone available to come and get you. I'm having a hell of a time locating someone. I don't know what the deal is. It could be hours—and you're a lot further out than I thought you were."

"I know," I grunted, shaking my head. "I don't know how the fuck we drifted this far out. I mean, don't get me wrong—" I sighed. "I *did* take us out farther than I intended to. That's on me. I just wanted her to have a good time."

"Well, I know she had a very interesting time during the storm. You're lucky that you didn't catch the storm head-on. All hands on deck with a search and rescue of another boat—came in before I talked to you though, so I wasn't worried."

"Yeah, well, I don't know how long we'll keep power, Jett. The generator isn't even working. There's nothing to charge the batteries. I don't know what we're going to do if we go dark."

"I have emergency lights in the storage," Jett said, his voice straining. "I can't believe the motor locked up. I knew it was bad, but I didn't think it was *that* bad. The moment that damn thing makes it back to the marina, I'm selling it. I don't even care what I get for it. I don't even care if it goes to the scrap yard."

"You could just put a whole new motor in it," I suggested, nearly laughing as he groaned.

"No way in hell am I gotta do that. I think the damn thing is doomed. I'm done with it."

"I wouldn't say it's doomed," I reasoned. "It kept us safe through the storm."

"Touché. But still. I'll keep you updated. Your dad already sent me information."

"All right," I said. "I'll be looking for your call."

We said goodbye and I hung up, slipping the phone into my pocket. I stepped out, taking a deep breath as I approached Layla, who didn't notice me.

"Okay, well, I love you, baby. Mommy will be home soon." Her voice sounded singsong, and I froze, my mind replaying what she had just said...

*Mommy.*

*She's a mommy.*

She set the phone down on the table, startling when she saw me standing there. Her eyes widened, her mouth dropping open as the air thickened. "Luke..."

"What the fuck..." My voice trailed off. "I think...you have something to tell me. *Now.*"

# 25

# Layla

"I..." My throat felt too tight to even spit the words out. "I'm sorry I didn't tell you," I managed to say.

"How many kids do you have?" Luke demanded, folding his arms over his chest. "I mean, I know we haven't talked a lot about the past, but come on, that's a *major* fucking detail to leave out about your life, Layla!"

"Why are you so mad at me?" I sputtered, jumping to my feet as his face reddened. "People have children all the time—and I only have *one*. I have a daughter."

"You have a daughter," he repeated, beginning to pace as he ran his fingers through his hair. "I can't even believe this..."

The way he was flying off the handle about me having a child completely threw me off guard. I mean, he didn't even *know* that she was his. "Luke, you have to let me explain..."

"Explain what? How babies are made? Because I'm well aware of how that works—are you even on birth control?"

My mouth dropped open at the question. "Yes! I am. I'm not stupid, Luke. I don't have unprotected sex." I couldn't believe he was picking at me like he was my parent or something. "I'm—"

"I just never really expected this to happen..." His voice trailed off.

"Why...why would you say that?" My bottom lip quivered, hurt searing through my chest. "I've only ever been with *three* people, Luke. I'm not some promiscuous woman. I've done nothing but focus on my career. Autumn was just...she was an accident, but she's the best thing that's ever happened to me," I said, his face softening at the name.

He shook his head. "I don't know...I don't even know what to say. It's just the fact that you kept it from me, Layla. Why wouldn't you tell me you have a daughter? Why would you hide that from me?"

"Well, obviously, you wouldn't have taken it well," I pointed out, folding my arms across my chest. "You literally asked me if I'm on birth control."

"Considering the fact that we had unprotected sex, I think that's a perfectly fine thing to ask," he spat out, his sharp tone returning. "And I'm sorry if that pisses you off, but I just...I don't want to have kids outside of a marriage."

*Well, that's just too damn bad.*

"It's not that I don't want them—or wouldn't be willing to accept someone who has them," he added quickly, running his hands over his face. "But it's the fact that you *hid* it from me! It just goes to show that you were never actually serious about this."

I raised my eyebrows, suddenly more irritated than hurt. "Not serious about this? Why the fuck *should I* be serious about this, Luke? We didn't work out the first time, and I was *never* good enough for you!" The words left my mouth, my tone painfully sad.

His jaw dropped in surprise, as if what I'd just said was some sort of shock to him. "Layla—"

"No," I snapped, holding up a hand to stop him. "I don't want to have this conversation right now with you. Obviously, now that I have a child, it's apparently changed things—and I get it, I do—but I don't wanna do this right now. I need space."

"Of course you need space," he sputtered, his anger returning. "Is that what it was in New York City six years ago? You just needed space?"

I shook my head. "I *said* I'm done talking about this. I left because I wasn't good enough after high school for you to tell your parents about us—so much so that you *broke up* with me—and I'm not good enough for you now. Just leave me alone." My voice was sharper than it had ever been, and he shut up, going silent as I stormed out of the captain's lounge.

I flung the door open and thundered up to the deck, welcoming the fresh air. Everything about Luke was fucking with my head, and there I had been, thinking that we would have a shot at making something work. My eyes flickered out to the dark waters, wondering what lay beneath the surface... Sharks? Dolphins? A sea monster?

A laugh slipped from my lips as I thought of the latter, a shiver rolling down my spine as I tucked my arms around myself. My phone buzzed in my hands, and I glanced down to see Delilah calling me. It was a miracle that I had service, and I knew it was just because of the Wi-Fi.

"Hello?" I answered, thankful for the distraction. I had no idea what Luke was doing, but he hadn't sounded happy while on the phone...and I hadn't had a chance to ask why...

*And won't be doing so, anyway.*

# LAYLA

"I was just calling to check on you." Her tone was heavy with concern. "I know Luke said the power may not last long. That'll cut off the ability to contact you unless it's through the satellite phone."

I hesitated, taking in the information. "What do you mean?"

"Uh..." Her voice trailed off. "I figured he was keeping you in the loop. The generator isn't working, so the batteries might die...and then the boat will go dark. That's what happens. We're trying to get someone out there to tow you in. The storm has just caused some problems because of the two shipwrecks."

"What? Shipwrecks?" The news just kept getting darker and darker.

"Jeez!" Delilah exclaimed. "Are you just not talking to Luke about anything? Because he knows all this. He called his dad to help pull some strings to get help out there faster. Are the two of you getting along?"

I frowned, now even more irritated with him than before. "Well, actually, it's been fine—actually, like really good—but then he...he overheard me on the phone telling Autumn goodnight and touching base with Lily."

"Oh my god..."

"Yeah..." I glanced around myself, making sure that Luke hadn't somehow snuck up on me again. "And he doesn't know that he's the father, either. He fucking flew off the handle just because I *have* a kid..."

"It's probably the fact that you didn't tell him," she reasoned. "He'll probably calm down about it."

"He asked me if I was on birth control," I groaned, facepalming. "You'd think that I had just gone out and done it on purpose."

"Girl...you *have* to tell him he's the father now," she said, letting out a heavy sigh. "That'll at the very least make him eat his words, which I think he should."

"I don't know..." I hesitated, my heart hammering with anxiety at the thought. I honestly should've just told him right there in the moment, but his over-the-top reaction had caught me off guard completely. "Maybe I should just go home as soon as we get back to shore. His brothers and dad are coming to Miami anyway. They're trying to buy some record label."

"Oh...that's intriguing," she said, as if it wasn't at all. "But that has nothing to do with you telling him the truth about who Autumn's father is. All it's going to take is a little bit of digging into you, and he's going to find out on his own."

"Yeah, I know," I grumbled. "But I might wait until we get back to shore before I tell him. I think that's probably the better time. I don't know if it's a good idea to stress him out even more."

"I don't know," she said carefully. "I think you might be better off to just go and tell him right now. Get it out of the way. You don't have to discuss it any further."

*Ugh.*

I took a deep breath, my eyes still focused on the seas. The warm lights on the deck were comforting, but my mind took the moment to taunt me with the image of what it might be like in total blackness. There was no moonlight, and while the stars were visible in the sky, there weren't nearly as many as usual. It was terrifying to imagine being engulfed by the darkness.

"I guess I'll let you go," I said, instead of agreeing to tell Luke about Autumn. I knew that more than likely she was right...and now that I'd had a few moments, I would find him and feel him out, seeing how he was acting about the entire thing. If he was still mad, it would just have to wait.

"Okay, well, you be safe. Jett is keeping in contact with Luke. If you don't wanna deal with it all, you might just go to bed. Let Luke handle it all. Maybe the power will last long enough for them to get there."

I nodded. "Yeah, for sure." I told her goodnight and hung up the phone, carrying it in my left hand as I headed back for the door. As I tugged on the handle, the lights flickered. My heart stuttered in my chest, and I ripped the door open, nearly running down the stairs and back to the captain's level.

"Luke!" I called as soon as I set foot in the lounge. I scanned the area, seeing no signs of him.

*Are there even any flashlights on this thing?*

I glanced around and headed for the cockpit, where I was hoping to find him...but he wasn't there either.

"Luke!" I shouted, my voice growing more strained as panic started to seep in. The lights flickered again, and a red light on the dash started blinking.

*Oh my god. We're going to lose power.*

My heart raced as I scoured the level, searching for any signs of Luke. I didn't know why the thought of being stuck in the dark was so damn terrifying, but it was...and all I could imagine was the sight of some massive boat crashing right into us. I trotted to the captain's room, ripping open the nightstands, searching for any sign of a flashlight.

Sure enough, I found one in the second drawer.

I grabbed it, holding it in my other hand and slipping back out into the lounge. As soon as I stepped out into the open, my eyes landed on Luke. He had shed his shirt, his body drenched in sweat.

"Where were you?" I demanded, his eyes dropping to the flashlight in my hand.

"I was getting the emergency lights set up on the deck and ready to power on. I think we're going to go dark." There was a concern in his voice that caused me to pause, suddenly forgetting that we had just had an argument over me being a single mom.

"Delilah told me on the phone that we were going to run out of power," I said, keeping my voice calm. "And she also said that it's taking so long for them to get out here because there was a shipwreck...people are missing."

"Yeah...I know. I didn't tell you because I didn't want to worry you, and I thought that maybe we'd be towed out of here before we lost power, but..." He hesitated, searching my face. "It doesn't look like that's going to happen. We're going to have to set up emergency lights. I have a satellite phone that will work—but we won't be able to use our cells anymore."

I nodded, my heart still hammering in my chest—now was *definitely* not the time to tell him that my daughter was *his* daughter too. "Okay."

"We're going to be fine. My dad said we should have someone out here soon..." Something in his tone made me think he was holding something back.

"How soon?" I demanded.

"I don't know...they have to find us."

# 26

# Luke

The guilt was overwhelming...but the need to be seen in the middle of the vast fucking ocean was a little more important at the moment. Apologizing to Layla for being blindsided about the fact that she had a kid would just have to wait...

And maybe I wasn't over it yet, anyway.

It wasn't that I was against single moms, but one, she'd kept it from me, and two... Fuck, I was jealous of whoever got to experience having a baby with her. For some reason, I had never imagined Layla having a family if it wasn't with me—and yeah, that was so incredibly selfish...

But I couldn't help it.

*I still love her.*

But what else was she hiding? Was that the only secret she was keeping from me? Or was there more? I shook my head, trying to rid my brain of the thoughts and focus on the task at hand.

We needed lights.

"Are you sure this is going to be enough for them to see us?" Layla questioned me as I started attaching one of the spotlights to the railing on the back deck.

I let out a sigh. "It's a toss-up, but they know our general location. It'll be better than nothing."

She nodded, holding one of the big lights in her arms. "I hope they get here soon."

My eyes took her in, seeing the weary look on her face. Her hair was pulled up now, with wispy strands falling around her face and neck. She was still wearing the same thing she had been earlier, and I wondered if Delilah had any spare clothes on board that she could borrow. She needed to get some sleep—I had no idea how long we'd be out here.

I turned my attention back to the task at hand, fastening the light to the railing and checking the batteries. I didn't know how long we had before rescue...but I would only run the lights through the night. If I thought too much about the timeline, it would start to psych me out. I'd grown up on boats, and I'd heard the stories. Even if they know your general location, it can take days to find you...

Or they never fucking find you.

*They're going to find us.*

My hands were steady as I finished zip-tying the lights to the rails. It was kind of ironic to be on a multimillion-dollar boat fastening spotlights with plastic ties. I chuckled to myself, eyeing Layla who made a weird face at me.

"I was just thinking how crazy it is that we're on such an expensive boat and having to rely on this." I held up the plastic bag of black zip-ties."

"I guess," she said with a shrug. "I guess luxury doesn't always mean reliability." There was something in her tone that caused me pause, but

I didn't read into it in the moment. I had a feeling it had something to do with me, and the last thing I wanted to do was fight.

We'd already done that, and I didn't want to go back.

"It'll be fine," I muttered, flipping the switch on the back of the light. A bright beam cast out, illuminating a narrow streak of water, but as bright as it felt, I knew it didn't cast out far.

Hopefully it would be far enough.

"So how many more of these do we have to do?" Layla asked as I headed to the other side of the deck, another light in my hand. "Like, is this really going to help?"

"I mean, it's either this or we rely on their spotlights to happen upon us," I reasoned. "And that's like trying to find a needle in a haystack. We're not *that* far off of shore, but yeah. I don't know."

Her lips fell in a straight line. "You don't sound very sure right now."

"Thanks for noticing," I grunted, shaking my head at her. "We're stranded in the fucking ocean, Layla. There's not a lot to be sure of." I met her gaze and she let me hold it for a few long seconds before she looked away, her eyes casting off across the dark waters.

"Do you think they're already heading to us?"

"No," I said honestly. "I don't think they are. The last time I talked to them, they were still trying to get to the marina. The storm caused some damage to some of the boats that were docked there. The guy who's supposed to tow us back took some damage. They're having to wait on backup."

"No way…"

I shrugged, trying to play it off like it hadn't bothered me when Jett told me. "It's all good. They'll get out here when they can. We have water and food. There are much worse boats to be stranded on."

"But the fridge can't run, so…"

"So I guess it won't be hard to catch," I joked, nearly laughing at the way she rolled her eyes. "But seriously, there are nonperishables in there. We'll be fine. I'm not worried about that."

"We don't have cell service anymore," she continued, wrapping her arms around herself.

"We have a satellite phone," I countered, doing my best to reassure her. "No, we can't go texting and making phone calls to everyone, but we can still communicate if there's an emergency."

"Like if the boat starts to sink." Layla's voice was flat, her steady expression unmoving.

I fought the urge to roll my eyes. "This yacht is a piece of shit, but it's not going to sink."

*Unless there's another bad storm.*

I pushed the thought away, continuing, "I really don't think you have much to worry about. They'll be here by morning, probably." I was talking out of my ass now, but I seriously didn't want her to worry about our well-being. That was my job.

"Okay, if you say so." She rocked almost in motion with the boat.

"Let's just focus on getting these lights rigged up, and then we can talk about the rest of our plan, okay?"

She nodded, falling into silence as I continued to install the lighting on all four sides of the boat. The last thing I needed was for us to be hit by a bigger ship—or smaller ship—all because they couldn't see us. It didn't happen that often, but if it did, it would be bad for us.

And probably them too.

Layla followed me around, holding lights or tools as I needed her to. She was being as helpful as she could be, and I appreciated her—and the fact that she was still willing to help even after I had been a total dick to her. I typically loved the ocean at night, always finding something almost magical in the way the stars shone a little brighter, and a whole world existed beneath the surface of the dark waters...

But being stranded was a completely different idea.

And I was not a fan of feeling as though the waters could swallow us up in an instant—or that the crew on shore might not make it to us in a few days. I kept telling myself that wouldn't happen, but with the other search and rescue mission going on, there was no telling when they'd make it to us.

"So now what?" Layla's voice caught my attention as we entered the captain's level, and I set down the remaining equipment and tools on one of the couches in the lounge. The luxurious yacht now felt eerie with just the light of the flashlights we held.

"I don't know," I said with a shrug. "You ought to get some sleep though. I'll probably just sit up on the main deck and keep watch." I couldn't really make out her expression, but she clicked her tongue in a way that sounded hesitant.

"I don't want to sleep down here. It's creepy as fuck."

"Valid point," I chuckled, glancing around. "Probably shouldn't go lighting any candles either. We'd really be out of luck if this thing caught fire."

She didn't think the joke was funny, not even acknowledging that I'd said anything at all. "I don't think they keep any candles on here."

"There's the fake ones," I pointed out, careful about recalling anything romantic between us. I didn't know where we were at in the moment, and my head was a fucking wreck, regardless. "But why don't you just grab a blanket and come up to the deck. You can sleep on one of the couches up there?"

"Yeah, I guess I could do that."

I nodded. "Okay, do you want me to wait for you?"

"No, I'll be fine. I don't think the boogeyman stowed away on the boat."

I laughed, finding the seriousness in her tone comical. "You never know. Maybe he sabotaged us. Got us stranded, and now he's going to strike."

She swatted my arm, her tone lightening up a little. "Don't scare me, Luke."

"Sorry," I chuckled, hating the tension rising between us. There was an elephant in the room, and there was no way we were going to be able to sweep it under the rug...but for now, I wouldn't press her. I would be the first to admit that I wasn't the best when it came to talking about hard shit...

And Layla having a kid was hard shit.

She disappeared into one of the rooms, and I headed for the stairs, fatigue starting to creep over my body as I climbed the steps to the deck. I was fucking exhausted, and as much as I wanted to shut my eyes and sleep, I couldn't. There was no way in hell I could. I had to keep my eyes peeled for any ships that might serve as a rescue. Hell, I'd be more than happy for just about anyone to tow us in.

I shut off the flashlight as I made it to the deck, glancing around at the luxurious couches and outdoor furniture. I remembered when Jett had purchased the yacht—it was his first big *striking-it-rich* kind of buy. I hadn't been around to help him, but even if I had, he'd have wanted to do it on his own. I didn't blame him. That's how I did everything.

On my own.

I tossed the flashlight onto one of the couches and moseyed out to the railing, looking out on the beam of light from the first spotlight I had hung. Gliding my hands against the cool metal railing, I gazed out at the black waters, wondering what lay beneath at that very moment...

"You okay?" Layla's voice startled me, but thankfully, unlike her, I didn't nearly fall over the railing.

"Yeah, just thinking about how many sharks are circling the yacht, waiting for us to fall in."

"Ha ha," she muttered, shaking her head. "They wouldn't want you if you fell in. You'd taste too salty."

I chuckled. "I deserved that."

She hesitated, the blanket wrapped up in her arms. "We should probably talk about that...I haven't—"

"Yeah, I owe you an apology for it, Layla." I took a step toward her, holding her gaze. "I was an asshole about it, but I was hurt that you didn't tell me about your daughter. I know you, and I know she's probably a big part of your life. It felt like you locked me out—and maybe that's because you don't want this to go anywhere."

"I didn't think it would go anywhere," she clarified, chewing on her bottom lip. "I *never* thought we'd be here discussing taking another chance on our relationship. I thought you were gone for good—and that's where my head has been this whole time."

I nodded, taking the gut punch with grace. "Yeah, things feel rocky between us, but you know as well as I do that we have something between us—and maybe it's just the fact that we grew up together and shared so many firsts—but it feels like more than that."

She nodded. "I know, and I should've mentioned my daughter...but I try to protect her from things. I never let her meet anyone I date—not that I ever date, really. I haven't been on a date in about a year. It never works out for me."

"Me, either," I said softly. "Because every time I try to make it work, I always just find myself wishing that it was you."

"Luke..." Her voice trailed off as she shook her head. "It's been ten years since we were together—and even now, looking back, I don't know if we were *actually* together." Her words cut like a knife, but I didn't show it.

"You should probably get some sleep," I choked out. "I need to keep watch."

She let out a sigh and retreated to one of the couches. It wasn't long before I heard light snoring coming from her, and I slid down, dropping my feet over the side of the yacht, under the railing. I leaned against the bottom rung, letting the support take some of the weight off my shoulders.

Too bad it didn't work to take the load off my fucking heart.

# 27

# *Layla*

I woke up feeling nauseous from guilt, my eyes adjusting to the potent darkness on the deck of the yacht. I knew I hadn't slept more than just a few hours, and I felt horrible that Luke probably hadn't gotten any shut-eye at all…and the fact that he *still* didn't know Autumn was actually his daughter. There had been no question about paternity at the time. I hadn't slept with anyone else in months.

Blinking my eyes, I shifted on the hard outdoor couch, an ache already beginning in my lower back. Ever since giving birth to Autumn, my lower back was prone to hurting, and it was always the first part of my body to grow sore. I rolled onto my back, the pain only worsening.

*Ugh.*

I flipped the blanket back and sat up, looking for Luke as I shifted. It didn't take me long to locate him. He was out at the railing, sitting with his legs dangling over the side, and it appeared his focus was out across the waters. A lump began to grow in my throat as I stood shakily to my feet.

*I need to just tell him and get it over with.*

He clearly wasn't mad about me having a kid anymore, and his initial reaction had been more knee-jerk than anything else. I was understanding of that. I pushed some of the loose hair behind my ear and adjusted my bathing suit, wishing I had something else—something more comfortable—to wear. My bare feet padded silently across the deck, but even still, Luke must've heard me coming.

"You should go back to sleep. It's only been a couple of hours," he said in a fatigued, flat tone. "It's probably going to be a while."

"Have you heard from anyone?" My voice was still heavy with sleep as I took a seat beside him, leaning against the railing to catch his eye.

He shook his head. "I have the phone with me, but no, I haven't had a call. I don't know if they even will call when they're on their way."

"So they could show up at any time," I reasoned, trying to lighten his mood. He was beyond tired, I could see it in the way his lips stayed in a straight line, and dark circles had begun to form around his eyes. I hated seeing him this way.

"They'll get here when they get here," he muttered, turning back to the ocean. "We might get lucky and see another ship pass by. I can probably signal to them that we need help."

"But the radio doesn't work."

"We have flares."

"Oh." I shrugged my shoulders, a shiver rolling down my spine as the salty breeze rolled across the water. "Hopefully it would be a nice boat that rescued us."

"You watch too many crime documentaries," he chuckled, shaking his head. "You've always imagined the darkest scenario when it comes to things."

"True," I laughed. "It's funny you know I still watch them."

"I didn't figure that was a habit that would change. I swear, there's something about women and loving that dark shit. It's weird."

"You're weird," I teased, nudging his shoulder.

He turned to me, raising a brow. "That was a terrible comeback."

"You're a terrible comeback," I laughed, a smile forming on my face as he joined me, chuckling at my shitty jokes—just like always. I leaned toward him, running my hand along his thick biceps. That familiar feeling between my thighs returned, and I tensed my legs muscles, borderline embarrassed at how easy Luke was able to turn me on...without even trying.

But he must've sensed it too, because before I knew it, his fingers were lacing through my hair, and my lips were crushed to his. I knew I should've stopped him and told him the truth about Autumn, but I didn't. Part of me was consumed with the thought that *this* might be the last time that I got to be with Luke in this way. I wanted to indulge in it, committing him to my memory before it was all over—and all we were was co-parents.

"Fuck," he groaned into my mouth as my kiss grew more desperate, the thought of it being the last time taking over. I sucked on his tongue, playing with it as I worked the buttons free on his shirt. His fingers were still in my hair, but I just wanted him naked so I could feel his skin on mine.

Luke shifted, letting me push the button-up shirt off his shoulders, tossing it toward the middle of the deck. I ran my hands over his bare chest, brushing against his taut muscles and stubble of hair there. Luke was the definition of masculine, his body chiseled and strong.

His arm threaded around my waist, pulling me away from the railing as he moved us closer to the center of the deck. I used the moment to go for his shorts, and he let me pull them off of him, his erection free.

"You're eager," he chuckled in a husky tone, helping me remove the cover-up. "I like it."

I gave him a lustful smile, hiding all the emotions welling up in my chest. I reached behind me, pulling the string of my bikini. My breasts dropped free, and his gaze dropped along with his jaw.

"I swear I never get tired of seeing your tits," he chuckled as I removed my top and tossed it to the side. He untied my bottoms on either side, letting the material drop. I climbed onto his lap, straddling him as Luke leaned forward and planted heady kisses on my chest. I moaned at the feeling of his tongue gyrating against my nipple and his thick cock teasing my pussy. I situated him between my legs, letting my natural lubrication cover his shaft.

I rocked my hips, pleasuring myself as his cock glided back and forth between my folds, allowing me to grind on him. "*Ooh...*" my voice rang out in a sultry tone, as pleasure built between my legs.

Luke groaned in response, sucking me further into his mouth as his hands traveled down my back, not stopping until they made it to my ass. He gripped it, hanging on to me as I continued to use his cock to pleasure myself.

I threaded my fingers through his light brown hair as he continued to kiss my body, his lips sending waves of pleasure straight to my core. My breaths became shallower and more labored as I edged closer to my climax, savoring every little thing about the moment...his scent, his touch, his hot breath on my skin...I didn't want to forget any of it.

"*Luke...*" I cried out just as I came, my eyes closing as the intense pleasure came in an intense wave. My body trembled against him, shivering as I clung to him, riding out the ecstasy until the very end.

His grip on my ass tightened as he pulled me forward, just enough to align himself with my entrance. Luke pressed into me, letting out a sharp breath as he plunged deep inside, stretching my pussy to fit his thick cock.

"Fuck, you're always so tight," he murmured into my shoulder as I began to ride him, grinding my hips against him. He pulled me close to him, our bodies pressed against each other beneath the moonlight. I slowed, my eyes locking with his as he wrapped me up in his arms.

"It's always been you." Luke's words broke my walls down, and the emotions bubbled up in my chest, forming a lump in my throat.

I blinked back the tears, leaning down to take his lips with mine. My tongue glided along his bottom lip, and I nipped at him. He growled back, taking my mouth possessively with his own.

His hands landed back on my ass, this time taking control of my movements. Luke worked my pussy against his cock, his strong arms doing all the work in the moment. I wrapped my arms around his neck, fisting the back of his hair as our kiss grew messier and heavier.

Excitement and pleasure began to build in my core again as he moved my hips in a sensual way, and my body threatened to release again. I moaned into his mouth as we clung to each other in the moment, and for the first time, I wondered if he thought this might be the last too.

Heartbreak, love, and need rushed through my veins as I felt more and more desperate for him, my arousal now mixed with raw emotion. I cried out his name in the night, my voice breathy as I gasped for air.

Luke moved his lips to my neck, sucking on my skin as he growled, his voice rattling in his chest. I shut my eyes, feeling the moisture pool behind my lids as I reached my orgasm. His body tensed against mine as I pulsed around him.

"Fuck, *I love you*," he muttered, the words shocking me as he came hard and fast inside of me. A rogue tear slipped down my cheek, and I batted it away before he could see ten years' worth of emotions funneling up and out.

But I didn't say it back.

As I came down, I couldn't shake the fear that maybe he was just saying it because of the intensity of the moment. After all, he still didn't know the truth...

And I wasn't sure he'd still want me once he did.

Our bodies stilled against each other, and I tried to breathe in deep, ignoring the tears rolling down my cheeks now. He kissed my neck tenderly, before bringing my face to his. I held my breath, wondering if he could see the stream of moisture coming from my eyes, but as his lips pressed to mine, the worry faded as did the tears.

As we finally broke apart, I quickly wiped my face, removing the evidence. I reached for my top, the reality of being totally exposed coming to my mind. I slipped it over my head and Luke helped me tie the back of it before getting dressed himself.

"So..." Luke cleared his throat after we were dressed again. "Tell me about your daughter."

I froze at the words, already knowing what I had to do next. "She's a really sweet girl," I began, taking a deep breath. "She's five."

He blinked a couple of times, but I couldn't read his face in the darkness. "When's her birthday?"

"November eleventh," I said carefully, not sure if he was putting it together or not. "She started kindergarten this year..."

He was quiet as we stood there, leaning against the railing. "What's her name?"

I braced, thinking of the name that he had always said he loved back when we were younger, dreaming of a future—but then again, maybe he wouldn't remember. "Autumn."

"Autumn," he echoed, a painful tone in his voice. He looked away from me again, his eyes drifting out to sea and staying there. "Is she staying with her dad right now?"

"No," I answered, letting out a sigh. "She's with my sister in New York while I'm here. She loves her cousin."

He nodded. "Is he...um." He paused, running his fingers through his hair. "Is the guy in her life?"

I bit my cheek. "Uh, no, not right now."

"Sounds like a piece of shit," he grumbled, shaking his head as his voice went sharp. "I don't know who would have a kid and not be in their life."

"Someone who didn't know she existed."

His head whipped back in my direction. "He doesn't know?" I could already see the judgment building in his expression. He was about to lecture me on how terrible it was for me to hide her—and I wasn't going to give him that chance.

"No, he doesn't know, because *he* is *you*."

"What?" Luke's face contorted in a mixture of hurt and anger. "What did you just say?"

"I said, *you* are Autumn's father." I kept my tone even. "And I should've told you a long time ago, but honestly, I wasn't good enough for you then, and I didn't want her to—"

"You got pregnant that night in New York?" he cut me off, his eyes wide. "What the fuck, Layla?" Luke's voice boomed in the still of the night. "You fucking got *pregnant* and you just what? Decided that you'd never tell me? Hide my daughter from me forever?"

I shook my head, taking a couple of steps back as the tears rolled down my cheeks. "You didn't want me!" I cried, my voice trembling. "That was the problem all along. I wasn't good—"

"We have a baby." He wasn't giving me the chance to talk. "We have a fucking *kid*, and she probably thinks her dad is a worthless piece of shit who doesn't care about her! I would've been there for her, Layla. I *should've* been there for her."

"Luke, I'm sorry, but I just...I was worried she—*we*—wouldn't be good enough for you."

"She's my *family*."

His words cut like a knife as I wrapped my arms around myself, knowing that he was right. Autumn was his family, and I shouldn't have kept her from him. It dawned on me in the moment that by default, Autumn was good enough for him.

Because she *was* a part of him.

"I can't believe you kept her from me," he repeated himself, looking at me with disbelief. "What about Jett? Does Jett know?"

"I think he has his suspicions, but I didn't want you to be with me just because I was pregnant..."

"But this isn't about you, Layla. This is about a child—*my* child—who I haven't ever even fucking met, because you *hid* her from me."

A heavy sob rattled my chest, and I was suddenly at a loss for words. I just wanted to get off the stupid boat and get away from him—and all the insecurities and heartbreak sweeping through me. I deserved the reaction he was giving me, but it only emphasized the fact that it would *never* work.

"You seriously have nothing to say?" he asked, shaking his head.

I looked up at him, seeing the anger in his eyes—and I was reminded of his indifference when he'd broken up with me. "You know," I began as I got myself back together, "I love you, Luke. And you might say that shit when you're inside of me, but you never *once* thought about the way you made *me* feel when you forced *me* to be a secret for nearly *three* fucking years. You broke up with me because I wasn't good enough for your family."

"Layla—"

"*No*," I cut him off. "Just *no*. You broke my heart, and you never once told me you were sorry. You ran off to your ivy league school and made a name for yourself—and it was like I never existed. You changed your fucking phone number." I squeezed my eyes shut as the painful memories flooded back. "And then we met in New York City by happenstance, you acted like nothing had happened between us. You never said sorry, and so yeah, I left because I was terrified that I would get my heart broken all over again. I found out I was having Autumn, and I thought about telling you, but then I figured, if it would've fucking mattered to you, you would've called me after that night."

Silence settled between us, and as it did, the sound of an engine filled the space. Luke opened his mouth to say something to me, but before he could, lights flooded the darkness...

And there was our rescue.

*Thank god.*

# 28

# Luke

I stared at Layla as she climbed on board the tow boat, while Jett climbed onto the yacht with me. My head was a fucking *wreck*. I mean, I'd thought things were a mess before, but now I was suddenly the father of a five-year-old little girl and I had no idea what she even looked like. I'd never seen her, met her, or even had the option of knowing she existed.

"This is wild," Jett laughed as he clapped his hand down on my shoulder. "Like holy shit, man. I thought there for a minute we weren't gonna find you before daylight set in. What a fuckin' nightmare."

"Yeah, crazy," I muttered, my eyes still on Layla. She had accepted the invitation onto the tow boat the moment it had been offered, and I knew it was to outrun my anger. But honestly, it was for the best at the moment. No matter how pissed I was at her, I had a daughter—and now that I knew about her, I *would* be in her life.

Layla would just have to deal with me.

"You okay?" Jett's voice sounded distant as Layla disappeared, probably heading into the cabin to rest. "I'm sure she just wants the Wi-Fi over there so she can let her sister know she's okay."

"And her daughter," I snapped, whipping my head to meet his shocked gaze. "But you already knew about her. Somehow, I was kept in the fucking dark all this time."

Jett's face dropped, and the guilt nearly caused me to come unglued. "Dude, I'm sorry..."

I shook my head. "Why would you fucking keep it from me? You *knew* I still had feelings for her!"

"It's not my place to tell you about her life," Jett shot back, leveling with me. "And you better get your shit together or I'll knock you right off the side of this boat. It was not our business nor our place to tell you about Autumn. If Layla wanted you to know, then she would've told you. But you act like you've been in her life all this time—and you were completely absent until this fucking vacation."

I shook my head. "She's *my* daughter."

"Fuck," Jett grumbled, running his hands over his face.

"You knew it," I growled through gritted teeth.

He let out a heavy sigh, heading under the covered area of the deck as the yacht lurched forward. "I didn't *know*, but I knew, if that makes sense," he said, plopping down on the couch that Layla had been sleeping on. "No one ever outright told me." His admission simmered my anger down a little, though it didn't go away completely.

"So she never told anyone who Autumn is then," I grunted, taking a seat beside him. "That's fucking rich."

Jett eyed me wearily. "I get why you're mad, I do, but come on, Luke. We've had this conversation before. You've never given Layla a reason to believe that you'd ever choose to be with her out loud."

"All this." I gestured around me, exasperated. "I've been trying to win her over, and every time I feel like it might happen, it all fucking goes wrong—or I find out I have a five-year-old daughter. That's a big fucking secret to keep hidden from me," I added, fury building back just at the thought. "It's just wrong. It's so wrong. I *loved* her."

"So what?" Jett raised his eyebrows. "Now you don't love her?"

"I never said that," I retorted, shaking my head. "I just know that I can't make it work with someone who hides things."

"But she told you?"

"She told me because I overheard her talking to her—and even still, she didn't tell me she was my daughter. She didn't tell me that until right before you guys showed up."

Jett nodded. "I'm sorry, man. I know it's a lot..."

"It's more than a lot. It's my entire life changing. Now that I know I have a daughter, I'm not going to skip out on being in her life, but she's *five years old*. I've missed *five* years of her life." The anger toward Layla shifted, and true heartbreak slipped into my chest as I thought about the little girl. "I don't even know what she looks like."

Jett shifted, pulling his phone out of his shorts pocket. "Here." He scrolled through his pictures, and my stomach knotted up as I waited, suddenly more anxious than ever. He stopped on a picture and handed the phone to me. "That was about a month ago."

I nodded, blinking back the emotion as my eyes landed on a little girl, her arms wrapped around Layla's neck as they stood with Delilah. "Man..." My voice trailed off, not even knowing what to say. She was beautiful, with Layla's green eyes...but she had my hair and skin tone, and my dimples.

"She looks so much like you," Jett said softly. "That's why I always thought maybe she was yours. I learned about the night in New York

City, and the math just added up…and you know, Layla isn't really one to sleep around."

I couldn't pull my eyes from Autumn, so many different emotions welling up in my chest. I was so incredibly angry at Layla for hiding her, but I was in so much awe that Autumn existed. I had a daughter…and I couldn't wait to know her.

Hell, I already loved her.

"I know it's a lot to take in," Jett continued as I ran my hands over my face. "And you have every fucking right to be angry with Layla. Hiding Autumn wasn't fair or right to you or Autumn—but it would probably be helpful for you to see her side."

I turned to Jett, my face flushing. "What side is there to see? Why do you *always* take up for her?"

Jett let out a sharp exhale. "Because you fucking dropped her like a fly."

"That was a *decade* ago!" I exploded. "Why the hell am I being put under fire for something I did when I was nineteen? My life was so different back then. My mom isn't even in my life anymore. I wanted to make it right with Layla when we ran into each other in NYC."

"So if that's how you really felt, Luke, why didn't you call her after she left that morning? You easily could've reached out. You could've said sorry, and maybe offered some sort of explanation for the way you broke her fucking heart. She doesn't trust you, and I don't blame her for that."

I shook my head, Layla saying that she wasn't good enough coming back to mind. "I get that what I did was shitty…but it was never about *her*. It was *me*. I was so wrapped up in trying to keep the peace with my family…and in the end, there was nothing I could do about it. There was nothing I could do to make my mom stay."

"No, and I don't fault you for doing what you did, no matter how shitty it was. You had a lot going on in your life, and I get that, but you still have to own up to the heartbreak that you caused."

"If I could go back, I would change it," I admitted, letting my mind wander back to the past. "And I would've loved her out loud. I was just dumb, and I guess when I look back at it all, I always just focus on the good. I don't let my head get hung up in the bad...which is why I thought that night in NYC was my chance to start over."

"Dude, you just have to tell her this stuff," Jett said, eyeing me. "And I know that's hard to do when you just found out she's been hiding a kid, but you both have shit to apologize for...and I don't think you should give up on Layla because of this. If you love her, don't give up. Maybe try to go at it all with a clean slate."

"That's impossible," I countered, leaning back against the couch as the sun began to rise on the horizon. "I don't know how to be with someone who did something like she did. I don't think I can do it."

Jett shrugged. "Well, then I guess you have to at least figure out how to be cordial with her, because you're going to be co-parenting with her. There's no getting around that. Not to mention, we live in LA right now, so you'll be flying across the country any time you wanna see her."

"I'll just move to LA." I shrugged. "It's not that big of a deal. Autumn is my daughter, and I'll make sacrifices for her—I would've if Layla had told me six years ago too."

"But why would she have been able to trust that you would tell your family about them?"

"Because my family had changed by then, and even if they hadn't, I would've changed regardless. I missed her like hell when we broke up, and I never let go of what we had."

# LUKE

"But now you're gonna let it go, right? Because you've said multiple times that you can't forgive her for what happened." Jett's eyes glanced down to the phone still in my hand, and I did the same, this time my eyes landing on Layla.

Her bright smile and green eyes looked back at me, and my heart stuttered, my mind flashing to the moment we had on the deck—before she'd admitted that Autumn was mine. Everything had been fucking perfect, and I could *feel* the love between us reigniting stronger than ever. In the moment, I had known that we were going to make another go...

*And I wasn't going to let her go this time.*

But that was *before* I'd found out that she hadn't just kept her daughter a secret, she had kept *my* daughter a secret. I had been able to rationalize why she might not tell me right off the bat that she was a single mom with a daughter. As much as it had hurt that she hadn't told me, it wasn't the end of the world...

However, hiding *my* daughter for five years?

That was a lot harder for my mind to come to terms with. She knew how to find me. She knew that I would want to be a part of their lives. So, why wouldn't she have told me? I couldn't see past it...

And I wasn't sure if I would ever be able to.

"This boat is a piece of shit," Jett muttered, his voice cutting through my thoughts. "Like, the biggest fucking piece of shit."

I nodded, chuckling. "Yeah, I'd say that you should consider getting rid of it—but I think you already know that."

Jett groaned. "Yeah, and to think I was planning to head to the Bahamas on this thing next year."

"I don't think I would trust this thing to make it out of the marina," I laughed, though my voice sounded strained. I hadn't fucking slept in almost twenty-four hours, and now my head was so wrecked, I wasn't sure I would be able to.

"Your dad and brothers are here," Jett commented, his voice dropping off again. "They're waiting at the resort."

"Fuck," I muttered, running my fingers through my hair. "I'll have to tell them about Autumn..."

"And Layla."

"Jackson already knows about Layla," I reasoned, meeting Jett's gaze. "But yeah, I'll explain everything to them. I'll have to have help with the custody arrangement with Layla."

Jett went silent, not offering up anything more on the subject. He wanted me to go apologize to Layla, confess my love, and somehow get some kind of fucking happy ending with her...but the pain was real and so was the betrayal.

"You should probably get some sleep once we make it back to shore," Jett said, clearing his throat. "It'll help you clear your head with everything that's happened in the last twenty-four hours. You look exhausted."

"I *am* exhausted." I rubbed my eyes, which had grown irritated and painful over the last couple of hours. "But I don't know if I'll be able to sleep."

Jett shrugged. "You should probably try. Might bring some clarity, and God knows you need that."

# 29

## Layla

"He hates me."

"Don't say that," Delilah said, reaching out and grabbing my hand as I threw my clothes onto the bed. I was already packing to leave for New York City. I wanted to be with Autumn. Luke could find me there—and I knew he would.

But I couldn't stay in Miami the way things were.

I knew that he was angry with me for all the right reasons, but I wasn't sure how long it would take him to cool off. I could only imagine how much the news was rocking his world.

"You know he'll get over it," Delilah spoke up while I kept shoving my clothes into my bag. "And I don't think it looks good for you to run, Layla."

I stopped, letting out a sharp breath. "I'm not *running*. I just need to get back to real life."

"That's not why you're leaving, and you know that. I know he's mad, but he's just trying to process everything. He's had a bombshell dropped on him."

"I know, I know." I let out a heavy sigh and plopped down beside her on the bed. "He just didn't even say a word to me when we made it back to the marina. It was like I didn't even exist."

"Like I said, he's just had a bombshell dropped on him. I'm sure he'll talk to you about it all eventually. Not to mention, neither of you have had much sleep. You were stranded at sea in the middle of a storm for heaven's sake."

I nodded, my head falling into my hands. I was beyond tired, not having slept other than the short span of a few hours on the boat. Maybe I wasn't thinking all that clearly.

Delilah's warm hand rubbed my back through my oversized T-shirt. "It will all work out the way it's supposed to, and it has to be a relief that you're no longer hiding Autumn anymore. It was a big secret. I can't imagine the weight that you carried for so long."

"Yeah, but I haven't even told Lily that he knows yet. She kept warning me to be careful and not fall for him again—but that's exactly what I did. I fell head over heels for him, thinking that we could try again...and that we could be some kind of family. But...I knew the truth would cause him to cut me off," I groaned into my hands before running my fingers through my hair. "I was such an idiot."

She hesitated, uncertainty filling her face. "So...you really think this is the end for the two of you? Because you're going to be seeing each other a lot more. If anything, I would think it *might* bring you together."

"We might see each other more, but I think I've ruined things with Luke. I did the right thing by telling him though," I thought aloud, reassuring myself. It would've been wrong to continue to pursue things with him and keep Autumn a secret. It never would've worked that way.

"You did, but I just don't think you should give up on the relationship with Luke. From everything Jett has told me, Luke really wanted to make a second go of the two of you. Like—" She let out a sigh. "Maybe he needs to cool off and think about how to go forward with everything."

"You literally go back and forth so much," I laughed, though I felt nothing close to humor.

"Well, to be honest, this is the most complicated relationship shit I've ever heard of." Delilah's eyes were bright as she said it, but her tone had an air of concern. "You'll work it out though. I know you will."

"Okay, but..." My voice trailed off. "I still think I'm going back to New York City. It's not like I'm flying back to LA."

"Do you think you'll move back to NYC once everything settles? I mean, I know that Luke has the money to fly back and forth, but logistically speaking..."

"I don't know." I didn't want to even think that far out. I knew that things would change for myself and Autumn...but that would require Luke to talk to me about it all—and he was avoiding me. Well, or at least he hadn't talked to me since getting off the boat a few hours ago.

"He's probably just sleeping," Delilah spoke up, like she was reading my mind. "And he might be pissed if he wakes up and you're gone."

"Okay," I huffed, tossing some of my clothes into my open suitcase. "So, I'll give him twenty-four hours. If he doesn't show up to talk to me about it all in one day from now, then I'm leaving. I'll book my flight back to NYC right now."

"Ballsy," Delilah laughed, shaking her head at me. "But I'm not gonna lie, I kind of like it. Giving him an ultimatum might not be so bad."

"I don't know," I muttered, not sure if it *was* the right thing to do. After all, I had been the one who kept his daughter a secret from him for nearly six years. I was starting to feel the repercussions of that now, and honestly...

I was feeling awful for it.

"Well, I think you should get some sleep in the meantime," Delilah said, pushing herself up off the bed. "It'll be good for you. Honestly, you need to think about how you want to go forward with it all too. It's not like you can just run off and introduce Luke as Autumn's father and it will all suddenly mesh like he's been in her life her whole life."

"You're preaching to the choir, Del."

She gave me a sympathetic look, opening her mouth to say something. However, before my best friend got any words out, there was a knock at the door. She raised her dark brows at me, giving me an *is that him* kind of look?

My heart jumped like I had taken off in a sprint as I walked to the door, anxiety rattling my chest. I tried to slow it down with some deep breaths, knowing that the lack of sleep wasn't helping anything. I peered through the peephole, and disappointment hit me like a tidal wave.

"Jett," I greeted him, swinging the door open. "What're you doing here?"

He gave me a weird look, stepping through the entrance. "Don't act like my wife isn't in here giving you some sort of therapy session. I know Luke, and I can only imagine just how angry he was with you."

I shrugged. "It was deserved."

He shook his head as he walked down the small hallway to where Delilah was standing, leaning against the dresser. "I don't know that I agree with you, Layla."

"You don't think it was wrong to hide Autumn from Luke?" Delilah seemed just as surprised as I felt.

"I don't know," he said, his eyes jumping between the two of us. "He hasn't exactly been the model citizen when it comes to your relationship, and you know, I know you hurt him after you left that night in NYC, but...he could've called you."

I chewed on my bottom lip, unsure of what to say. I didn't *disagree* with him, but I wasn't sure that I agreed either. "It was wrong to hide Autumn from him—you should've seen how hurt he was."

"Sure, but it's not like he's some kind of fucking saint," he snapped, letting out a sharp breath. "I just don't want him to mess this up because he's angry about it."

"I take it he must've said some awful things about me," I muttered, my eyes dropping to my hands.

"No, he didn't say anything that bad about you." Jett's voice softened. "He loves you, Layla. I know he does. He has for years. He's just...he's just got a lot to process with it all. I just hope he doesn't blow it before he really thinks about it."

"Well, he hasn't said anything to me since we got back to shore," I said carefully, wondering if Jett had been with him.

"He went to sleep," Jett grunted. "He's got some fucking business meeting tomorrow that he's got to get prepared for. You know his brothers and dad are here, right?"

I shook my head, my heart sinking deep in my chest. The thought of his family—the people he hid me from—made my stomach sick. "Will he tell them that I hid Autumn from him all these years?"

Jett shrugged. "Hell if I know."

I felt the urge to cry all over again. "They're going to think I'm a horrible person. What if they want to take her from me?"

Delilah rested her hand on my shoulder. "They're not going to do that. It wouldn't be good for Autumn."

"They're not nearly as bad as you think they are," Jett added, running his fingers along his jaw. "Luke has never said a bad word about *you*. He's not going to do that to his family—I don't think, anyway. They aren't the same family they used to be. His mom is long gone, and she was the one who pushed him so damn hard."

"It'll be fine," Delilah reassured me, pulling me into a hug as a fresh tear rolled down my cheek. "It's all going to work out the way it's supposed to."

I tightened my arms around her, leaning on my best friend. I still had to break the news to Lily, and I was dreading it. "I should probably get some sleep."

"Yeah." Delilah pulled away, giving me a soft smile. "I'll see you later. Just call me when you get up. I'll be there as soon as you need me."

I nodded. "Thanks. I don't know what I'd do without you."

"Goodnight, Layla," Jett said with a nod, grabbing Delilah's hand and walking her toward the door.

"Night, guys." I shut the door behind them, locking the chain lock before turning around and heading back toward the bed. It was covered in a mess of clothes, and as I stared at it all with fresh eyes, I realized just how emotionally charged I was in the moment.

*I do need to get some sleep.*

I grabbed my bag and set it on the floor, filling it with the rest of the clothes that had surrounded it on the bed. I scooted it to the side and flipped back the covers, climbing in between the sheets. Reaching for my phone on the nightstand, I checked for any notifications, including any texts from my sister.

I had let her know that I'd made it to shore, and that I needed to talk to her as soon as she had time. However, I knew that she was sleeping, and I didn't want to call and wake her up. I had lessened the entire yacht escapade, not wanting her to worry about it—or ask a lot of questions.

Laying my head back on the pillow, I held the phone up, scrolling to Luke's name. I clicked on it, my fingers hovering over the keyboard. I wasn't sure if sending him something would make it a lot worse or help...

*Ugh.*

"I'll just tell him that I'm leaving tomorrow," I said to myself, but then shook my head. Maybe it was better if I didn't say anything at all. Jett and Delilah were right; more than likely he was taking the time to process things...

*But his family is here...*

Was that why he hadn't said anything to me once we landed? He used to go dark when he spent time with his parents, and the whole thing felt like déjà vu.

And it terrified me.

# 30

## Luke

"The finances are solid," Eli said, picking up his glass of water as we sat around the table.

I hadn't touched any of the food in front of me, my entire body feeling numb from the previous night. I knew I still had to talk to Layla about it all, but at the moment...I didn't even know what to fucking say to her. Part of me wanted to wrap her up in my arms and tell her that I'd do whatever it took to make the *three* of us a family...

But the other part of me was still angry and hurt.

"What do you think about it?" Jackson kicked me under the table, and I jerked my eyes up from the plate full of my shrimp linguini. It was nearly two o'clock and I had slept a solid ten hours. The shrimp linguini was basically my breakfast, and I was not a fan...of any food at the moment.

"I think that I wouldn't choose to buy the company if it wasn't something you wanted," I admitted, my voice strained. I sounded like

# LUKE

I hadn't slept in five days, but I didn't care—not even about the weird looks they were giving me.

"What the hell is wrong with you?" Eli asked, his brows furrowing. "You haven't been yourself since you showed up to lunch."

I shrugged. "Just the whole stranded at sea thing."

"You were out there for less than twenty-four hours," Dad chuckled, eyeing me. My dad was young for having kids our age, but that was because he and mom had us when they were young—and somehow, despite my dad being fifty years old, he was often mistaken for being ten years younger.

"Is it Layla?" Jackson asked me, my heart thudding a little extra hard at the mention of her name. "Did being stranded at sea freak her out?"

"Layla?" Eli and my dad both asked simultaneously, giving me a look.

"Who is Layla?" Dad added, his face full of curiosity. "Did you meet someone here?"

I ignored the bright, chipper tone of his. "Uh...kind of."

"It's Layla Miller," Jackson clarified, rolling his eyes at me.

"Oh?" A bright smile stretched across Dad's face. "I remember her. She was such a sweet girl. Always liked her."

I shifted uncomfortably in my seat, not sure what to say. There was so much more to the story than what they *all* knew—now including Jackson. I had thought coming clean to him about my past with Layla had been hard enough...

But now I had a five-year-old daughter I had never met.

"You dating her?" Eli questioned as an awkward silence settled between us all. "Because you're acting really fucking weird, man."

"He *did* date her," Jackson blurted, bursting into a fit of laughter.

"What?" Dad turned to me, tilting his head. "I don't understand. Last time we talked you weren't seeing anyone—and you said you haven't seen anyone in years..."

"Yeah, because I haven't," I muttered.

"So then when did you date her?" Dad was looking more and more confused. "I feel like you would've told me about her."

I shot Jackson a glare before turning back to my father—now was the time to tell them all about it. "I dated her all of high school."

"What?" His eyes went wide. "Why didn't you ever tell us?"

I shrugged. "You know how Mom was..."

He nodded, sympathy filling his face. "Oh shit, son."

"She's the reason he wanted to go to UCLA," Jackson chimed in. Usually, his loud mouth was annoying, but in *this* moment it was welcomed, saving me from having to explain it all.

"Damn..." Eli's voice trailed off. "No wonder you were so depressed when you came to school. That's tough... Why did you hide her? Just because of Mom?"

I nodded, running my fingers through my hair. "You know how she was, and you know what happened when I told her I wanted to go to UCLA."

"Yeah, I wish I could go back and change that for you..." The regret in my dad's bright blue eyes made me feel even worse about what I still had yet to tell them all.

"So you rekindled the romance here?" Eli asked, forking a bite of his fish. "I think that's pretty cool. You think she's the one or something?"

I shrugged. Eli had changed his outlook so much since marrying Olivia, and I had to admit that I was jealous of him...but my head was still swimming with confusion when it came to Layla. Before I knew that she had hidden my daughter from me, I would've answered with confidence that she was...

# LUKE

But fuck, I was still hurting.

"Son?" My dad's hand squeezed my shoulder. "You look upset."

"Did she call it off?" Jackson furrowed his brow.

I shook my head. "I have no idea. I don't know where we stand at all." I had been mulling over it all and thinking about what Jett had said about her. I wanted it to be easy—to forgive her and move forward—but I was feeling stuck on it.

"So...what is it then? Is she not sure if she wants to try again?" Eli cocked his head to the side. "I'm sure you broke her heart when you broke up all those years ago—I can't imagine the pain of hiding a relationship too."

"Yeah...but it's not that." I chose my words carefully. "It's something much, much more serious..."

Everyone fell silent at the table, and I could tell they were waiting for me to tell them what it was. I reached for my water, suddenly feeling parched. I gulped some of it down, the moisture not doing anything for my cotton mouth.

"What is it?" Jackson urged. "We're on the edge of our seats here."

I took a deep breath. "We met up about six years ago in NYC, and everything felt the way it used to, you know? It's like nothing had changed...and things went a little too far..."

"Uh...we know how the birds and the bees work, bud." Jackson burst into a fit of laughter. However, Eli and my dad had no signs of amusement on their faces. They'd caught on to what I was saying.

"I have a five-year-old daughter, and I *just* found about her...*last night*." The words made my stomach lurch, my mind replaying the tears streaming down Layla's face as she apologized over and over.

"Whoa..." Jackson's smile faded. "What the hell, man? So, you had no idea?"

I shook my head. "No, I had no clue at all. I guess she...I guess she just assumed that I wouldn't want anything to do with her or the baby."

"That's *quite* an assumption," Dad commented, his lips forming into a frown. "To hide a child from their father is...*wrong.*"

I nodded, wanting to jump into agreement with him. However, guilt crept in, reminding me of the heartbreak I had brought her. "I...I don't know. It's not that simple between us. I never called her after that night. I thought because she left early that night, that she didn't want anything to do with me. But in reality, she was just still reeling from everything that had happened when we broke up—she never thought she was good enough because I hid our relationship..."

"And then dumped her," Jackson added in a chiding tone. "Brutal."

"But she still should've told you about the baby," Dad cut in. "I get that there was a lot of hurt, but you're talking about another human being—who isn't getting to know her father because of it."

"Yeah, but you know, Olivia didn't tell me she was pregnant," Eli reasoned. "And I don't hold that against her. Things weren't good for us, and she wasn't sure if I was serious about her. She didn't want me to be with her because of that, and at first it was hard to understand, but I get it now. I'm glad I made it right with her."

I swallowed, the lump growing in my throat. "I don't know what I'm going to do. I just know that I want to be a part of my daughter's life."

"But how did you feel about Layla before you found out?" Jackson asked, grabbing up his tea. "I think you're avoiding that aspect of your relationship."

I shook my head. "I just don't know what to think about that. I'm angry and hurt that she betrayed me like that."

"She didn't *betray* you," Eli snorted, shooting me a hard glance. "You're being too hard on her. You weren't together and you weren't even talking to each other, so why would she tell you? Maybe she thought that it'd just be sympathy if you chose to be with her after that...and *maybe* you didn't give her a reason to think you'd be there for her. She spent her entire time with you thinking that you weren't proud to be with her. I could see the damage that would cause."

"You have a point." Dad's face softened. "I guess I never thought about it like that. Maybe if you'd reached out, she would've told you. It's now been six years, and maybe she thought that you would just be a fleeting moment in her life this time too."

*Damn...*

"I've come across like a real asshole," I muttered, my eyes dropping to my hands. "And I never apologized for what happened all those years ago."

"So maybe that's why she's so reluctant," Dad commented, letting out a sigh. "So...had you not found out about having a daughter, what would you have wanted from all this?"

I hesitated. "What is this? A therapy session?"

"Don't blow off the question, son," Dad scolded me. "You're talking about your *future*, and it affects the life of your daughter—whether you know her right now or not."

"I love Layla." I choked out the words, fighting back the emotions that were forming a lump in my throat. "And she's the only woman I've ever wanted to be with for a long time—or seen a future with."

"So why not pursue that?" Dad asked. "I get that she didn't tell you about your daughter, but if you love her, you have to think hard. This might be the last chance you have to make things right between the two of you."

"Three of you," Eli added, giving me a look. "You think Layla is the one, don't you?"

"I did, yeah," I said carefully. "But my head is a fucking wreck now. I don't know what I'm supposed to do. She lied to me…"

"No, she just didn't *tell* you. Did you ask her if she had kids? Did you ask her who the father was?" Eli leveled with me, his tone growing sharp. "I get you're mad and hurt, but that shit fades faster than you think. You don't want to ruin it and then regret what you did later when you see her happy with someone else."

"I need to talk to her," I said, letting out a sharp breath. "And maybe start out with apologizing for everything that happened in the past."

"I think that's a good idea," Eli said, giving me a smile. "Don't let her go if you've spent all these years wishing that you would've spent them with her."

"I agree," Dad said in a light tone. "And maybe while we're all here, we could meet her, and get reacquainted—show her that we would've accepted her right into the family. We're not those kind of people…not anymore," he added, his voice thick with emotion. "And it makes me sad to think that we *were* ever those people."

"Yeah, so go." Jackson shooed me from the table. "We don't have to have an offer on the record label until next week. Get the fuck out of here and go get your lady."

I laughed, pushing myself back from the table, shaking my head. "You guys are ridiculous, but yeah, okay." I bid my family goodbye and headed out of the restaurant, a whole new urgency awakening in my chest.

As soon as I made it out into the open air, I pulled out my phone, hoping Jett knew where she had gone.

"You're a little late," Jett said, his tone distraught. "Layla's gone."

"Wait, what?" I stopped in my tracks, unable to process what I was hearing. "Why the hell would she have left?"

"Because you never talked to her about it, ignored her text, and she figured you needed a lot of space. Her plane leaves in forty-five minutes."

"What text?" I ripped my phone away from my ear, putting the phone on speaker. "I haven't gotten a text..." But as soon as I pulled open the thread of messages, I saw the missed text from her...*hours* ago.

*Can we talk now, please?*

"Oh, fuck," I said, exasperated. "I have to fix this."

# 31

# Layla

My foot tapped anxiously as I slid into the back of the car, shutting the door as I did. The text to Luke had gone unanswered for hours, and I knew he had seen it by then. At first, I thought he was just still sleeping, but Jett had told me he'd gotten up and left for a meeting with his family...

So there was no question that he was ignoring me.

"Are you okay?" The Uber driver met my gaze in the rearview mirror, her bright red lipstick shimmering in the afternoon sunlight.

I forced a smile. "I'm fine, thank you."

She shook her head at me, her graying curls bouncing on her shoulders. "I can tell when someone isn't okay. I just want to make sure that you know someone is here for you."

"Thank you," I muttered, touched by the stranger's kindness, but also worried that it was *that* obvious I wasn't in the best shape. I smoothed out my dark hair, which was in a natural state, falling in waves past my shoulders.

# LAYLA

"Everything always works out the way that it's supposed to," she said, her gentle words not making me feel that much better. It sounded like an inspirational quote that I might read on Instagram, and it was *not* what I wanted to hear.

But I just stayed quiet.

My mind was all over the place as she pulled away from the resort, and I found myself unsure of whether or not I was making the right decision to go back to New York City. I didn't want Luke to think I was running, but being here with him avoiding me—even if it was just a day—was more than I could take. I wanted to hug my daughter...

And I wasn't sure Luke would come around while in Miami anyway.

For all I knew, he could be planning to leave for New York at the same time that I was. I let out a sigh, leaning against the car door and taking in the last sights of the palm trees and sandy beaches I would be seeing for now. There was a chance that I wouldn't be going back to LA, opting to stay in New York. I had already been considering it to be closer to Lily and my family, but honestly...

*Luke* was the reason I hadn't.

The city was a big place, but somehow, six years ago, I had still managed to run right into him—and I hadn't been able to risk that before. If he saw Autumn, he'd know...

But now he knew.

"Have a nice flight," the driver said to me as she set my bags on the sidewalk outside of the airport drop-off.

"Thank you." I forced another smile, reaching for the handle of my luggage.

She gave me one last nod as I entered through the sliding doors, leaving the salty sea air behind me.

After making it through hellacious security, I made my way to my gate, situating myself in the corner to keep watch. As I leaned against the handle of my bag, planning to check it last minute, my phone began to ring in my purse. My heart skipped a beat as I pulled it out, part of me hoping that it was Luke. However, it wasn't…

"Hey, Lily," I answered, already bracing for what she had to say.

"So, you're coming back early?" The air of suspicion in her tone told me she already had a good idea. "What did he do?"

"He knows," I said softly, trying to hold back my emotions. "I told him, and he didn't take it very well."

"Oh my god…" Her voice trailed off. "Why? Why did you tell him, Layla? You've kept her a secret for years…I can't even imagine how big of a shock that was for him."

"It was a big one, yeah, and we argued about it…kind of…" I didn't even know how to get the words out. "I thought that there might've been something between us still, but I think I ruined it." My voice broke as I said the last words, guilt and heartbreak searing through my chest.

"You didn't ruin it," Lily said, her voice soft. "I know why you feel that way, I do…but…if he wants to work it out, he will…"

"He said I betrayed him," I sniffled, biting back the sob threatening to explode in my chest. "And I feel so awful about it."

"He betrayed you too, if you want to go there. He didn't even tell you he was leaving for some ivy league school until the week before—all that time, he was never planning on going with you."

"That was *ten* years ago, Lily," I reasoned, suddenly feeling like I was the one in the wrong for holding that against him. "We were just kids."

"Maybe, I don't know. Your history is complicated, but if you want it to work, then you have to tell him when you talk to him—*if* that's what you want."

"That's all I've wanted," I finally admitted to both Lily and myself. "He's all I've ever wanted, and I don't know how I'm supposed to move forward with him in my life...but not with me."

"Are you sure this is what you want to do then?" Lily asked me, her voice thick with concern on the other side of the phone. "Because maybe he just needs a little more time to think about it all...maybe you should wait and hear him out—or go hunt him down and talk to him about it all. Don't run just because it's the easier thing to do, Layla."

"He *lives* in New York City," I argued, part of me wanting him to chase me. "I need to get away from all this...I don't just want to be home with you all. And I can't think here. I just can't think."

"I know..." Her voice trailed off. "I'm just worried it will make him even more angry about it all. He's just reeling from everything. I would be too..."

My eyes drifted to the boarding time, which was only twenty minutes from now. "I tried to text him earlier today, and he never even responded. His family is here, and I just..."

"It's okay, Layla." Her voice softened. "Just make sure you *tell* him where you're going, you know? I think that's probably the right thing to do. He needs to know that you're not running."

I squeezed my eyes shut, feeling a rogue tear slip down my cheek. "Okay, I'll let him know."

"Okay," Lily said. "Text me when you're boarded."

"Got it," I sniffled. "I'll text you then."

"It'll all work out the way that it should," she said just before hanging up. I stared at the phone for a few more long moments, wondering if I should call Luke or just send him a text. I tapped my foot anxiously, my stomach churning as I brought up his number.

I clicked the call button and put the phone up to my ear. "Please answer," I whispered, my heart hammering in my chest.

"Layla?" His voice sounded much softer than I expected.

"I'm going back to New York." I choked out the words just as a finger tapped my shoulder. I was startled, turning around to see Luke standing there behind me, the phone up to his ear.

"I don't want you to go to New York, Layla," he began, his eyes glassy with moisture as he held my gaze.

I blinked back the tears, surprised by the difference in his demeanor. "I know we need to talk about Autumn."

He shook his head. "No, right now we need to talk about *us*. We have to talk about Autumn, yeah." He choked up. "But *we* are the reason that she's here, you know?"

I nodded, all of the emotions coming to a head at his words. Tears spilled down my cheeks and he reached for me, pulling me into his arms.

"I'm sorry," he muttered, kissing the top of my head. "And I've owed you that *sorry* for a fucking decade."

I shook my head, leaning away from him. "I think I should be the one saying sorry. I hid her from you, and I shouldn't have. There's really no excuse for it."

"I should never have hidden you from my family, and I should've been with you instead of running off to the other side of the country. I'm sorry for the way things happened—and I'm sorry that I didn't give that apology to you sooner. I'm sorry that I didn't call you after you left...I am." His apology, though about ten years late, only made the tears come faster, soaking Luke's shirt. "I love you, Layla. I've always loved you, and I'll always continue to love you. It's always gonna be you for me."

I squeezed my eyes shut, clinging to him as they called for my flight to board. "I love you...but I'm gonna miss my flight," I choked out, leaning back to meet his gaze.

"Miss your flight," he said softly. "Miss your flight and come back to the resort with me. Let me introduce you to my family the way I should've years ago. *Please.*"

My eyes widened, fear pulsing through my veins. "Do...do they know?"

He nodded. "I told them everything about us today. Well, my brother already knew about us, but yeah."

"He already knew?"

"Yeah." Luke let out a sigh, chuckling. "I told him about the way I hid you from the family, and all that. He encouraged me to chase you. And I promise, if you're willing to give us a chance, I'll always chase you, Layla. Always." He wiped the tears from my cheeks. "And I'll love you out loud," he nearly whispered, leaning down and planting a soft kiss on my lips.

I deepened the kiss, sucking his tongue into my mouth as his grip tightened around me. He groaned lightly before pulling away and grabbing my bags.

"Let's go. They're waiting on us to get back, and I'm pretty sure they're fucking dying to meet you."

"Really?" I laughed, sniffling as I fell in step with him. "They don't even really know me."

"Yeah, but they know what you mean to me, and that's everything, Layla." He stopped me, meeting my gaze. "You—and Autumn—are *everything*. I want to do what it takes to make this work...if you're willing to."

I reached up on my tiptoes, planting a kiss on his jaw. "Yes, and I love you. Besides, you know what they say, right?"

"What's that?" he chuckled.

"Third time's a charm."

# Epilogue – Luke

## Six Months Later

"Daddy!" Autumn shouted as she bounded down the stairs of our Upper East Side townhouse, a smile on her face. "When are we going to the party? I'm *so* ready to go."

I took in the sight of her in her little red party dress, her caramel locks curled neatly and framing her face. "We're leaving soon, honey. Just waiting for Mommy." I gave her a smile, my foot tapping anxiously against the floor.

A big night was ahead of us, and I was terrified, the ring burning a hole in my pocket. I had bought it the week we'd gotten back to New York City, before I had ever even met Autumn for the first time. I just...*knew*.

"What's the party for?" Autumn asked me, huffing as she stepped off onto the floor and took my hand. "Because Aunt Lily said that it was a surprise, and I love surprises, but she said that it's not for me...it's for Mommy."

I laughed, squeezing her hand. "Well, it *is* for Mommy, but it affects you too. I think it'll be a good thing, and I think you'll be super excited about it."

"Mommy has a surprise for you too." Autumn grinned, looking up at me. She wiggled her eyebrows at me, like she was taunting me with information...

And something about it made me nervous.

"What is Mommy going to surprise me with?" I asked her, keeping my voice cool and collected. "Do *you* know what it is?"

"No," she said with a shrug. "Well, not really. But I heard her telling Aunt Lily that it was going to change everything. It's a big secret, though."

"Oh?" I cleared my throat, inching closer to the stairway. However, before I could make it to the stairs, the doorbell chimed.

*Damnit.*

I led Autumn to the door, peering at the monitor, seeing Eli and Olivia standing at the doorway. I opened the door, giving them both a smile as Autumn cheered.

"Hi, hi, hi!" She bounced up and down, grabbing ahold of Olivia's hand and dragging her into the townhouse. "Are you ready for the party, Aunt Ollie?" She had decided that Olivia's nickname would be Ollie, and luckily, Olivia went with it.

"Where's your mom?" Olivia asked as Autumn led her toward the living room. "Is she ready to go yet?"

"No, not yet," Autumn laughed, plopping down on the couch. "She takes *forever* sometimes."

"You ready for tonight?" Eli asked me, shooting me a wink. "Crazy to plan an engagement party before you've even popped the question."

# EPILOGUE - LUKE

"I know, I know," I said, bobbing my head up and down. "But I know that she'll want to celebrate with everyone."

"Yeah, it's gonna be a good night. We've already loaded the place out with champagne."

"Great," I laughed, shaking my head. "Just keep it away from Autumn. It's supposed to be a kid-friendly party, remember?"

"Yeah, yeah," Eli chuckled. "Ours will be there once Dad gets himself around. He's had *way* too much fun watching the kids."

I laughed. "Sleepovers with Grandpa seem to be a lot more fun than when we lived there."

"No kidding."

"I'll be right back. I'm gonna check on Layla really quick," I said, dipping out and heading toward the stairs. I thundered up the steps, not stopping until I reached the second floor. I headed toward the master bedroom, where I could hear the water running.

"Hey, baby," I called to her, ignoring the little pang of anxiety in my chest. I was worried what surprise she had for me, and what it could mean...

*Maybe she's going to propose to me.*

I laughed to myself as I stepped into our room, taking in the sight of Layla in a black dress, stopping just above her knees. Her dark hair trailed down the open back, showing off her creamy skin.

"You look beautiful," I said, smiling as I met her sultry eyes in the mirror. "Stunning, really. Makes me wanna take that dress right off you."

She smiled, her burgundy lips tempting my mind with all the things I'd like to do with her—to her. "You're sweet, and handsome," she teased, a smile on her face.

"So..." I began, leaning against the doorway. "Autumn told me you had a surprise for me."

Her shoulders slumped. "Ugh, did she really? Because I swore I kept her out of the room when I was on the phone with Lily."

"On the phone with Lily about what?" I countered, narrowing my eyes as I stepped further into the bathroom with her. "What's the surprise?"

"Well…" Her voice trailed off. "I wasn't planning on telling you anything yet…not until after tonight."

"And why after tonight?" I asked, folding my arms across my chest. "Why would you wait until after some silly little party?"

She laughed, shaking her head at me. "Is that all tonight is? Some silly little party, Luke?"

"Maybe," I said with a shrug. "I don't know what Jackson has up his sleeve. You know how he can be. He's wild."

"You're so full of it," she giggled, spinning around to face me. However, her smile faded as she ran her hand down my chest, her touch warm through my dress shirt.

I grabbed her hand, bringing it to my lips, kissing her skin softly. "What's going on in that beautiful mind of yours, Layla?"

She looked up at me, her eyes meeting mine—and filling with moisture. "I just…I have something to tell you."

My heart stuttered. "And what's that?"

"I…" Her voice trailed off as she took a long, deep breath. "I'm pregnant, Luke."

My mouth dropped open, emotion flooding my chest. "No way…"

"Yes way…" She gave me a slight smile. "Yeah, I found out this morning. I think Autumn overheard me telling Lily—and Lily told me to wait until after the party to tell you."

I laughed, wiping the tears from my eyes. "Holy shit, I'm so excited." I pulled her into me, kissing the top of her head. "We're gonna be a family of *four*."

"Yeah," she sniffled, leaning back to look up at me. "Two kids."

"Autumn will be the best big sister," I chuckled. "Well, unless she treats our baby the way she does her baby dolls. She drops them a lot."

"Oh stop." Layla swatted my chest, though she didn't stop giggling.

*Layla*

"You know she does though." Luke laughed, leaning my chin back. His lips brushed mine lightly, and I knew that he was avoiding messing up my lipstick. "And now it's time for me to tell you what *your* surprise is."

"What?" I furrowed my brows, confused by his words. "What are you talking about? Is that the party tonight? An early birthday surprise or something?" My birthday was still two weeks away, and I assumed maybe that was why Lily was telling me to wait until after the party.

But now I wasn't so sure.

"Layla, you know that we've been making a go of things," he began, letting out a sharp sigh. "And it's really been working out."

I nodded, my heart jumping at the beginning of his speech—one that sounded a lot like it might lead to something else. "I've loved every second of it," I said, squeezing his hand as he backed away.

"Yeah, and we have an *amazing* daughter," he continued, his voice thickening with emotion. "And I am *so* stoked for a second amazing kid with you...which is why I think the time to ask you is right now."

"Ask me what?"

He smiled, dropping down to his knee as he reached into his pocket. "Well, Layla Marie Miller, I have loved you for over a decade—though I've been an idiot for a lot of it. But I won't be an idiot anymore," he chuckled, laughing. "Will you marry me?"

I choked back the tears as I nodded. "Of course I'll marry you." The tears slipped down my cheeks as he slid the ring onto my finger. "It's *gorgeous*, Luke."

"Not nearly as gorgeous as you," he said softly, standing to his feet. He pulled me into him, his lips crushing to mine. I kissed him with all my force, and he groaned into my mouth, his hands slipping below my waist.

He squeezed my ass as I rubbed against him, feeling his arousal already. "How long do we have before we have to go?" he murmured into my ear as his lips caressed my neck, making his way lower. "Because I'd like to have a quick celebration."

"Mmm…" I moaned as his fingers trailed around the hem of my dress, playing with it as he sucked on the skin of my neck. "I don't know how long we have," I panted, arousal building between my legs.

"I can be so fast," he growled into me, his hot breath tickling my skin. "I'd love to be so fucking deep inside of you right now."

"Oh my god," I whimpered, just as he slid his hand up my dress. His fingers teased my black satin thong, already growing moist for him.

"All these years and you still get so wet for me," he murmured, pressing his hard shaft against my lower stomach. "It's so fucking addictive."

"You're addictive," I panted, pressing my body against him. "But I don't think we have time."

"Sure we do." He lifted his eyes to mine, searching them. "I'll always have time for you. Besides, I already did what the whole damn party was for."

I laughed, shaking my head at him. "Well, *they* don't know that."

"No, but they'll know as soon as they see that rock on your finger, baby." He leaned in, kissing my neck again. Excitement jolted through my body, and I nearly gave in, his fingers brushing against my center.

## EPILOGUE - LUKE

"Mommy! Daddy!" Autumn's voice called from the other side of the door, while her fist beat on the door. "We're going to be late! And Daddy is supposed to ask you to marry him!"

We froze, exchanging a glance, and then burst into laughter. I shook my head, already imagining that someone had given the secret away to her. Autumn was *not* who you let listen to your conversations if you wanted them to be private.

"Come on!" she whined, finally opening the door and stepping into the room. Her brows were furrowed, and her arms were folded across her chest, a look of impatience riddled her expression...

And I couldn't help but laugh even harder.

"What is so funny?" she demanded, shifting her hands to her hips.

About that time, Olivia appeared, an apologetic look all over her face. "Oh my gosh, I am *so* sorry! I tried to get her to just stay downstairs and watch TV, but she was really determined to go—and to know why we were having the party..."

"So I told her." Eli peered into the room, a sheepish smile on his face. "It's totally my fault...you can kill me now."

I held up my ring finger, shaking my head. "No need for that. He already asked me."

"What?" Eli burst into laughter. "We're throwing a massive party and you just asked her in the bathroom of your house? Dude, I could've saved so much money on champagne."

"You should've done that anyway," I said, shrugging my shoulders as I met Olivia's bright blue eyes.

Her mouth dropped open. "No way!"

"Yes way." I smiled as both Autumn and Eli looked more confused than ever. "You're going to be a big sister, Autumn, and I think we should celebrate that tonight as well."

Her green eyes went wide. "I get a baby brother?!"

"Uh...or a baby sister?" Luke offered, shaking his head as she launched toward us and right into Luke's arms.

I smiled at the two of them, my heart feeling full at the sight. It had been a bumpy ten years...and nothing about us was normal.

But it was right.

It was definitely right.

# About the Author

I'm an indie author who writes steamy romance that begs to be read cover to cover.

Bad boy alphas, grumps with a heart of gold, and high levels of steam are my specialty. Every sizzling book ends with a deliciously satisfying happily ever after.

Each book in the series can be read as a standalone, but the books are interconnected through the characters.

When I'm not writing, you can probably find me sipping wine and binge-watching reality TV, baking up a storm in my tiny kitchen, traveling with my family, or contemplating getting another dog, or cat. Or both.

See my other books on Amazon!

Printed in Great Britain
by Amazon